BEHOLDEN TO THE THRONE

BY

CAROL MARINELLI

First published in Great Britain 2013
by Mills & Boon, an imprint of Harlequin (UK) Limited.
Large Print edition 2013
Harlequin (UK) Limited, Eton House,
18-24 Paradise Road, Richmond, Surrey TW9 1SR

© Carol Marinelli 2013

ISBN: 978 0 263 23183 0

Harlequin (UK) policy is to use papers that are natural,
renewable and recyclable products and made from
wood grown in sustainable forests. The logging and
manufacturing process conform to the legal environmental
regulations of the country of origin.

Printed and bound in Great Britain
by CPI Antony Rowe, Chippenham, Wiltshire

For Penny Jordan,
who made me fall in love with sheikhs.
Rest in peace, Penny.
Loved, missed and always remembered.
C xxx

CHAPTER ONE

'SHEIKH King Emir has agreed that he will speak with you.'

Amy looked up as Fatima, one of the servants, entered the nursery where Amy was feeding the young Princesses their dinner. 'Thank you for letting me know. What time—?'

'He is ready for you now,' Fatima interrupted, impatience evident in her voice at Amy's lack of haste, for Amy continued to feed the twins.

'They're just having their dinner...' Amy started, but didn't bother to continue—after all, what would the King know about his daughters' routines? Emir barely saw the twins and, quite simply, it was breaking Amy's heart.

What would he know about how clingy they had become lately and how fussy they were with their food? It was one of the reasons Amy had requested a meeting with him—tomorrow they were to be handed over to the Bedouins. First they would be immersed in the desert oasis and then they would be handed over to strangers for the night. It was a tradition that dated back centuries, Fatima had told her, and it was a tradition that could not be challenged.

Well, Amy would see about that!

The little girls had lost their mother when they were just two weeks old, and since his wife's death Emir had hardly seen them. It was Amy they relied on. Amy who was with them day in and day out. Amy they trusted. She would not simply hand them over to strangers without a fight on their behalf.

'I will look after the twins and give them dinner,' Fatima said. 'You need to make yourself presentable for your audience with the King.' She ran disapproving eyes over Amy's pale blue robe, which was the uniform of the Royal Nanny.

It had been fresh on that morning, but now it wore the telltale signs that she had been finger-painting with Clemira and Nakia this afternoon. Surely Emir should not care about the neatness of her robe? He should expect that if the nanny was doing her job properly she would be less than immaculate in appearance. But, again, what would Emir know about the goings-on in the nursery? He hadn't been in to visit his daughters for weeks.

Amy changed into a fresh robe and retied her shoulder-length blonde hair into a neat ponytail. Then she covered her hair with a length of darker blue silk, arranging the cloth around her neck and leaving the end to trail over her shoulder. She wore no make-up but, as routinely as most women might check their lipstick, Amy checked to see that the scar low on her neck was covered by the silk. She hated how, in any conversation, eyes were often drawn to it, and more than that she hated the inevitable questions that followed.

The accident and its aftermath were something she would far rather forget than discuss.

'They are too fussy with their food,' Fatima said as Amy walked back into the nursery.

Amy suppressed a smile as Clemira pulled a face and then grabbed at the spoon Fatima was offering and threw it to the floor.

'They just need to be cajoled,' Amy explained. 'They haven't eaten this before.'

'They need to know how to behave!' Fatima said. 'There will be eyes on them when they are out in public, and tomorrow they leave to go to the desert—there they must eat only fruit, and the desert people will not be impressed by two spoiled princesses spitting out their food.' She looked Amy up and down. 'Remember to bow your head when you enter, and to keep it bowed until the King speaks. And you are to thank him for any suggestions that he makes.'

Thank him!

Amy bit down on a smart retort. It would be wasted on Fatima and, after all, she might do better to save her responses for Emir. As she turned to go, Clemira, only now realising that she was being left with Fatima, called out to Amy.

'Ummi!' her little voice wailed. 'Ummi!'

She called again and Fatima stared in horror as Clemira used the Arabic word for mother.

'Is this what she calls you?'

'She doesn't mean it,' Amy said quickly, but Fatima was standing now, the twins' dinner forgotten, fury evident on her face.

'What have you been teaching her?' Fatima accused.

'I have *not* been teaching her to say it,' Amy said in panic. 'I've been trying to stop her.'

She had been. Over and over she had repeated her name these past few days, but the twins had discovered a new version. Clemira must have picked it up from the stories she had heard Amy tell, and from the small gatherings they attended with other children who naturally called out to their mothers. No matter how often she was corrected, Clemira persisted with her new word.

'It's a similar sound,' Amy explained. But just as she thought she had perhaps rectified the situation, Nakia, as always, copied her sister.

'Ummi,' Nakia joined in with the tearful protest.

'Amy!' Amy corrected, but she could feel the disgust emanating from Fatima.

'If the King ever hears of this there will be trouble!' Fatima warned. 'Serious trouble.'

'I know!' Amy bit back on tears as she left the nursery. She tried to block out the cries that followed her down the long corridor as she made her way deep into the palace.

This meeting with the King was necessary, Amy told herself, as nerves started to catch up with her. Something had to be said.

Still, even if she *had* requested this audience, she was not relishing the prospect. Sheikh King Emir of Alzan was not exactly open to conversation—at least not since the death of Hannah. The walls were lined with paintings of previous rulers, all dark and imposing men, but since the death of Emir's wife, none was more imposing than Emir—and in a moment she must face him.

Must face him, Amy told herself as she saw the guards standing outside his door. As difficult as this conversation might be, there were things that needed to be said and she wanted to say them before she headed into the desert with the King and his daughters—for this was a discussion that must take place well away from tender ears.

Amy halted at the heavy, intricately carved doors and waited until finally the guards nodded and the doors were opened. She saw an office that reminded her of a courtroom. Emir sat at a large desk, dressed in black robes and wearing a *kafeya*. He took centre stage and the aides and elders sat around him. Somehow she must find the courage to state her case.

'Head down!' she was brusquely reminded by a guard.

Amy did as she was told and stepped in. She was not allowed to look at the King yet, but could feel his dark eyes drift over her as a rapid introduction was made in Arabic by his senior aide, Patel. Amy stood with her head bowed, as instructed, until finally Emir spoke.

'You have been requesting to see me for some days now, yet I am told the twins are not unwell.'

His voice was deep and rich with accent. Amy had not heard him speak in English for so very long—his visits to the nursery were always brief, and when there he spoke just a few words in Arabic to his daughters before leaving. Standing there, hearing him speak again, Amy realised with a nervous jolt how much she had missed hearing his voice.

She remembered those precious days after the twins had been born and how approachable he'd been then. Emir had been a harried king, if there was such a thing, and like any new father to twins—especially with a sick wife. He had been grateful for any suggestion she'd made to help with the tiny babies—so much so that Amy had often forgotten that he was King and they had been on first-name terms. It was hard to imagine that he had ever been so approachable now, but she held on to that image as she lifted her head and faced him, determined to reach the father he was rather than the King.

'Clemira and Nakia are fine,' Amy started. 'Well, physically they are fine...' She watched as his haughty face moved to a frown. 'I wanted to speak to you about their progress, and also about the tradition that they—'

'Tomorrow we fly out to the desert,' Emir interrupted. 'We will be there for twenty-four hours. I am sure there will be ample time then to discuss their progress.'

'But I want to speak about this well away from the twins. It might upset them to hear what I have to say.'

'They are turning one,' Emir stated. 'It's hardly as if they can understand what we are discussing.'

'They might be able to...'

Amy felt as if she were choking—could feel the scar beneath the silk around her neck inflame. For she knew how it felt to lie silent, knew how it felt to hear and not be able to respond. She knew exactly what it was like to have your life discussed around you and not be able to partake in the conversation. She simply would not let this happen to the twins. Even if there was only a slight chance that they might understand what was being said, Amy would not take that risk. Anyway, she was here for more than simply to discuss their progress.

'Fatima told me that the twins are to spend the night with the Bedouins…'

He nodded.

'I don't think that is such a good idea,' Amy went on. 'They are very clingy at the moment. They get upset if I even leave the room.'

'Which is the whole point of the separation.' Emir was unmoved. 'All royals must spend time each year with the desert people.'

'But they are so young!'

'It is the way things have long been done. It is a rule in both Alzan and Alzirz and it is not open for discussion.'

It hurt, but she had no choice but to accept that, Amy realised, for this was a land where rules and traditions were strictly followed. All she could do was make the separation as easy as possible on the twins.

'There are other things I need to speak with you about.' Amy glanced around the room—although she was unsure how many of the guards and aides spoke English, she knew that Patel did. 'It might be better if we speak in private?' Amy suggested.

'Private?' Emir questioned. His irritation made it clear that there was nothing Amy could possibly say that might merit clearing the room. 'There is no need for that. Just say what you came to.'

'But…'

'Just say it!'

He did not shout, but there was anger and impatience in his voice, and Emir's eyes held a challenge. Quite simply, Amy did not recognise him—or rather she did not recognise him as the man she had known a year ago. Oh, he had been a fierce king then, and a stern ruler, but he had also been a man sensitive to his sick wife's needs, a man who had put duty and protocol aside to look after his ailing wife and their new babies. But today there was no mistaking it.

Amy was speaking not with the husband and father she had first met, but to the King of Alzan.

'The children so rarely see you,' Amy attempted, in front of this most critical audience. 'They *miss* seeing you.'

'They have told you this, have they?' His beautiful mouth was sullied as it moved to a smirk. 'I was not aware that they had such an advanced vocabulary.'

A small murmur of laughter came from Patel before he stepped forward. 'The King does not need to hear this,' Patel said. Aware that this was her only chance to speak with him before they set off tomorrow, Amy pushed on.

'Perhaps not, but the children do need their father. They need—'

'There is nothing to discuss.' It was Emir who terminated the conversation. Barely a minute into their meeting he ended it with a flick of his hand and Amy was dismissed. The guards opened the door and Patel indicated that she should leave. But instead of following the silent order to bow her head meekly and depart, Amy stood her ground.

'On the contrary—there's an awful lot that we need to discuss!'

She heard the shocked gasp from the aides, felt the rise in tension from everyone present in the room, for no one in this land would dare argue with the King—and certainly not a mere nanny.

'I apologise, Your Highness.' Patel came over to where Amy stood and addressed the King in a reverential voice. That voice was only for the King—when he spoke to Amy Patel was stern, suggesting in no uncertain terms that she leave the room this very moment.

'I need to be heard!'

'The King has finished speaking with you,' Patel warned her.

'Well, I haven't finished speaking with *him*!' Amy's voice rose, and as it did so, it wavered—but only slightly. Her blue eyes blinked, perhaps a little rapidly, but she met the King's black stare as she dared to confront him. Yes, she was nervous—terrified, in fact—but she had come this far and she simply could not stay quiet for a moment longer.

'Your Highness, I really do need to speak with you about your daughters before we go to the desert. As you know, I have been requesting an audience with you for days now. On my contract it states that I will meet regularly with the parents of the twins to discuss any concerns.'

It appalled her that she even had to request an appointment with him for such a thing, and that when he finally deigned to see her he could so rapidly dismiss her. He didn't even have the courtesy to hear her out, to find out what she had to say about his children. Amy was incensed.

'When I accepted the role of Royal Nanny it was on the understanding that I was to *assist* in the raising of the twins and that when they turned four...' Her voice trailed off as once again

Emir ignored her. He had turned to Patel and was speaking in Arabic. Amy stood quietly fuming as a file—presumably *her* file—was placed in front of Emir and he took a moment to read through it.

'You signed a four-year contract,' Emir stated. 'You will be here till the twins leave for London to pursue their education and then we will readdress the terms, that is what was agreed.'

'So am I expected to wait another three years before we discuss the children?' Amy forgot then that he was a king—forgot her surrounds entirely. She was so angry with him that she was at her caustic best. 'I'm expected to wait another three years before we address any issues? If you want to talk about the contract, then fine—we will! The fact is the contract we both signed isn't being adhered to from your end!' Amy flared. 'You can't just pick and choose which clauses you keep to.'

'Enough!'

It was Patel who responded. He would not let his King be bothered with such trivialities. He summoned the guard to drag her out if required, but as the guard unceremoniously took her arm to escort her out, Amy stood firm. The veil covering her hair slithered from its position as she tried to shake the guard off.

It was Emir who halted this rather undignified exit. He did not need a guard to deal with this woman and he put up his hand to stop him, said something that was presumably an instruction to release her, because suddenly the guard let go his grip on her arm.

'Go on,' Emir challenged, his eyes narrowing as he stared over to the woman who had just dared to confront him—the woman who had dared suggest that he, Sheikh King Emir of Alzan, had broken an agreement that bore his signature. 'Tell me where I have broken my word.'

She stood before him, a little more shaken, a

touch more breathless, but grateful for another chance to be heard. 'The twins need a parent…'

He did not even blink. 'As I said, my role is to assist in the raising of the twins both here in the palace and on regular trips to London.' Perhaps, Amy decided, it would be safer to start with less emotive practicalities. 'I haven't been home in over a year.'

'Go on,' he replied.

Amy took a deep breath, wondering how best to broach this sensitively, for he really was listening now. 'The girls need more than I can give them—they…' She struggled to continue for a moment. The twins needed love, and she had plenty of that for them, but it was a parent that those two precious girls needed most. Somehow she had to tell him that—had to remind him what Hannah had wanted for her daughters. 'Until they turn four I'm supposed to *assist* in their raising. It was agreed that I have two evenings and two nights off a week, but instead—'

He interrupted her again and spoke in rapid Arabic to Patel. There was a brief conversation between the aides before he turned back to her. 'Very well. Fatima will help you with the care of the children. You will have your days off from now on, and my staff will look into your annual leave arrangements.'

She couldn't believe it—could not believe how he had turned things around. He had made it seem as if all she was here for was to discuss her holiday entitlements.

'That will be all.'

'No!' This time she did shout, but her voice did not waver—on behalf of the twins, Amy was determined to be heard. 'That isn't the point I was trying to make. I am to *assist*—my job is to *assist* the parents in the raising of the children, not to bring them up alone. I would never have accepted the role otherwise.' She wouldn't have. Amy knew that. She had thought she was entering a loving family—not one where children,

or rather female children, were ignored. 'When Queen Hannah interviewed me...'

Emir's face paled—his dark skin literally paled in the blink of an eye—and there was a flash of pain across his haughty features at the mention of his late wife. It was as if her words were ice that he was biting down on and he flinched. But almost instantaneously the pain dispersed, anger replacing it.

He stood. He did not need to, for already she was silent, already she had realised the error of her ways. From behind his desk Emir rose to his impressive height and the whole room was still and silent. No one more so than Amy, for Emir was an imposing man and not just in title. He stood well over six foot and was broad shouldered, toned. There was the essence of a warrior to him—a man of the desert who would never be tamed. But Emir was more than a warrior, he was a ruler too—a fierce ruler—and she had dared to talk back at him, had dared to touch on a subject that was most definitely, most painfully, closed.

'Leave!'

He roared the single word and this time Amy chose to obey his command, for his black eyes glittered with fury and the scar that ran through his left eyebrow was prominent, making his features more savage. Amy knew beyond doubt that she had crossed a line. There were so many lines that you did not cross here in Alzan, so many things that could not be said while working at the palace, but to speak of the late Queen Hannah, to talk of happier times, to bring up the past with King Emir wasn't simply speaking out of turn, or merely crossing a line—it was a leap that only the foolish would take. Knowing she was beaten, Amy turned to go.

'Not you!' His voice halted her exit. 'The rest of you are to leave.'

Amy turned around slowly, met the eyes of an

angry sheikh king. She had upset him, and now she must face him alone.

'The nanny is to stay.'

CHAPTER TWO

THE *nanny*.

As Amy stood there awaiting her fate those words replayed and burnt in her ears—she was quite sure that he had forgotten her name. She was raising his children and he knew nothing about her. Not that she would address it, for she would be lucky to keep her job now. Amy's heart fluttered in wild panic because she could not bear to leave the twins, could not stand to be sent home without the chance to even say goodbye.

It was that thought that propelled her apology.

'Please…' she started. 'I apologise.' But he ignored her as the room slowly cleared.

'Patel, that means you too,' Emir said when his senior aide still hovered, despite the others having left.

When Patel reluctantly followed the rest and closed the door, for the first time in almost a year Amy was alone with him—only this time she was terrified.

'You were saying?' he challenged.

'I should not have.'

'It's a bit late for reticence,' Emir said. 'You now have the privacy that you asked for. You have your chance to speak. So why have you suddenly lost your voice?'

'I haven't.'

'Then speak.'

Amy could not look at him. Gone now was her boldness. She drew in a deep breath and, staring down, saw that her hands were pleated together. Very deliberately she separated them and placed her arms at her sides, forced her chin up to meet his stare. He was right—she had the audience she had requested. A very private, very intimidating audience, but at least now she had a chance to speak with the King. On behalf of

Clemira and Nakia she would force herself to do so while she still had the chance. Amy was well aware that he would probably fire her, but she hoped that if he listened even to a little of what she had to say things might change.

They had to.

Which was why she forced herself to speak.

'When I was hired it was on the understanding that I was to assist in the raising of the children.' Her voice was calmer now, even if her heart was not. 'Queen Hannah was very specific in her wishes for the girls and we had similar values...' She faltered then, for she should not compare herself to the late Queen. 'Rather, I admired Queen Hannah's values—I understood what she wanted for her girls, and we spoke at length about their future. It was the reason why I signed such a long contract.'

'Go on,' Emir invited.

'When I took the job I understood that her pregnancy had made the Queen unwell—that it might take some considerable time for her to recover and that she might not be able to do all she wanted to for the babies. However—'

'I am sure Queen Hannah would have preferred that you were just *assisting* her in the raising of the twins,' Emir interrupted. 'I am sure that when she hired you, Queen Hannah had no intention of dying.' His lip curled in disdain as he looked down at Amy and his words dripped sarcasm. 'I apologise for the inconvenience.'

'No!' Amy refused to let him turn things around again—refused to let him miss her point. 'If Queen Hannah were still alive I would happily get up to the twins ten times in the night if I had to. She was a wonderful woman, an amazing mother, and I would have done anything for her...' Amy meant every word she said. She had admired the Queen so much, had adored her for her forward thinking and for the choices she had made to ensure the happiness of her girls.

'I would have done anything for Queen Hannah, but I—'

'You will have assistance,' Emir said. 'I will see that Fatima—'

She could not believe that he still didn't get it. Bold again now, she interrupted the King. 'It's not another nanny that the twins need. It's *you*! I am tired of getting up at night while their father sleeps.'

'Their father is the King.' His voice was both angry and incredulous. 'Their father is busy running the country. I am trying to push through a modern maternity hospital with a cardiac ward to ensure no other woman suffers as my wife did. Today I have twenty workers trapped in the emerald mines. But instead of reaching out to my people I have to hear about *your* woes. The people I rule are nervous as to the future of their country and yet you expect me, the King, to get up at night to a crying child?'

'You used to!' Amy was instant in her response. 'You used to get up to your babies.'

And there it was again—that flash of pain across his features. Only this time it did not dissipate. This time it remained. His eyes were screwed closed, he pressed his thumb and finger to the bridge of his nose and she could hear his hard breathing. Amy realised that somewhere inside was the Emir she had known and she was desperate to contact him again, to see the loving father he had once been returned to his daughters—it was for that reason she continued.

'I would bring Queen Hannah one of the twins for feeding while you would take care of the other.'

He removed his hand from his face, and stood there as she spoke, his fists clenched, his face so rigid and taut that she could see a muscle flickering beneath his eye. And she knew that it was pain not rage that she was witnessing, Amy was quite sure of it, for as sad as those times had been still they had been precious.

'And, no, I don't honestly expect you to get up at night to your babies, but is it too much for you to come in and see them each day? Is it too much to ask that you take a more active role in their lives? They are starting to talk...'

He shook his head—a warning, perhaps, that she should not continue—but she had to let him know all that he was missing out on, even if it cost her her job.

'Clemira is standing now. She pulls herself up on the furniture and Nakia tries to copy—she claps and smiles and...'

'Stop.' His word was a raw husk.

'No!' She would not stop. Could not stop.

Amy was too upset to register properly the plea in his voice, for she was crying now. The scarf that had slipped from her head as she made her case unravelled and fell to the floor. She wanted to grab it, retrieve it, for she felt his eyes move to her neck, to the beastly scar that was there—her permanent reminder of hell—but her hands did not fly to her neck in an attempt to cover it. She had more important things on her mind—two little girls whose births she had witnessed, two little girls who had won her heart—and her voice broke as she choked out the truth.

'You need to know that things are happening with your children. It is their first birthday in two days' time and they'll be terrified in the desert—terrified to be parted from me. And then, when they return to the Palace, they'll be dressed up and trotted out for the people to admire. You will hold them, and they will be so happy that you do, but then you will go back to ignoring them…' She was going to be fired, Amy knew it, so she carried on speaking while she still could. 'I cannot stand to see how they are being treated.'

'They are treated like the princesses they are!' Emir flared. 'They have everything—'

'They have *nothing*!' Amy shouted. 'They have the best clothes and cots and furniture and jewels, and it means nothing because they don't have *you*. Just because they're gi—' Amy stopped herself from saying it, halted her words, but it was already too late.

'Go on.' His words invited her but his tone and stance did not.

'I think that I have already said enough.' There was no point saying any more, Amy realised. Emir was not going to change at her bidding. The country was not going to embrace the girls just because she did. So she picked up her scarf and replaced it. 'Thank you for your time, Your Highness.'

She turned to go and as she did his voice halted her.

'Amy…'

So he did remember her name.

She turned to look at him, met his black gaze full on. The pain was still there, witness to the agony this year must have been for him, but even as she recognised it, it vanished. His features were hardening in anger now, and the voice he had used to call her changed in that instant.

His words were stern when they came. 'It is not your place to question our ways.'

'What *is* my place?'

'An employee.'

Oh, he'd made things brutally clear, but at least it sounded as if she still had a job—at least she would not be sent away from the twins. 'I'll remember that in future.'

'You would be very wise to,' Emir said, watching as she bowed and then walked out, leaving him standing for once alone in his sumptuous office. But not for long. Patel walked in almost the second that Amy had gone, ready to resume, for there was still much to be taken care of even at this late stage in the day.

'I apologise, Your Highness,' Patel said as he entered. 'I should never have allowed her to speak with you directly—you should not have been troubled with such trivial things.'

But Emir put up his hand to halt him. Patel's words only exacerbated his hell. 'Leave me.'

Unlike Amy, Patel knew better than to argue with the King and did as he was told. Once alone again Emir dragged in air and walked over to the window, looking out to the desert where tomorrow he would take the twins.

He was dreading it.

For reasons he could not even hint at to another, he dreaded tomorrow and the time he would spend with his children. He dreaded not just handing them over to the desert people for the night, but the time before that—seeing them standing, clapping, laughing, trying to talk, as Amy had described.

Their confrontation had more than unsettled him. Not because she had dared to speak in such a way, more because she had stated the truth.

The truth that Emir was well aware of.

Amy was right. He *had* got up at night to them when they were born. They *had* pulled together. Although it had never been voiced, both had seemed to know that they were battling against time and had raced to give Hannah as many precious moments with her babies as they could squeeze in.

He looked to his desk, to the picture of his wife and their daughters. He seemed to be smiling in the photo but his eyes were not, for he had known just how sick his wife was. Had known the toll the twins' pregnancy had taken on her heart. Six months into the pregnancy they had found out she had a weakness. Three months later she was dead.

And while Hannah was smiling in the photo also, there was a sadness in her eyes too. Had she known then that she was dying? Emir wondered. Had it been the knowledge that she would have but a few more days with her daughters that had brought dark clouds to her eyes? Or had it been the knowledge that the kingdom of Alzan needed a male heir if it was to continue? Without a son Alzan would return to Alzirz and be under Sheikh King Rakhal's rule.

He hated the words Hannah had said on the birth of their gorgeous daughters—loathed the fact that she had apologised to him for delivering two beautiful girls. His heart thumped in his chest as if he were charging into battle as silently he stood, gave his mind rare permission to recall Hannah's last words. The blood seared as it raced through his veins, and his eyes closed as her voice spoke again to him. 'Promise you will do your best for our girls.'

How? Emir demanded to a soul that refused to rest.

Any day now Rakhal's wife, Natasha, was due to give birth. The rules were different in Alzirz, for there a princess could become Queen and rule.

How Rakhal would gloat when his child was born—especially if it was a son.

Emir's face darkened at the thought of his rival. He picked up the two stones that sat on his desk and held them. Though they should be cool to the touch the rare pink sapphires seemed to burn in his palm. Rakhal had been a prince when he had given him this gift to *celebrate* the arrival of the girls—a gift that had been delivered on the morning Hannah had died.

Hannah had thought them to be rubies—had really believed that the troubles between the two kingdoms might finally be fading.

Emir had let her hold that thought, had let her think the gift was a kind gesture from Rakhal, even while fully understanding the vile message behind it—sapphires were meant to be blue.

Without a male heir the kingdom of Alzan would end.

Emir hurled the precious stones across his office, heard the clatter as they hit the wall and wished they would shatter as his brain felt it might.

He hated Rakhal, but more than that Emir hated the decision that he was slowly coming to. For it was not only Hannah who had begged for reassurance on her deathbed—he had held his dying father out in the desert. He had not been able to see the King dying because blood had been pouring from a wound above Emir's eye, but he had heard his father's plea, had given his solemn word that he would do his best for his country.

Two promises he could not meet.

Emir knew he could keep but one.

His decision could not—*must* not—be based on emotion, so he picked up the photo and took one long, last look, tracing his finger over Hannah's face and the image of his girls. And then he placed it face down in a drawer and closed it.

He could not look them.

Must not.

Somehow he had to cast emotion aside as he weighed the future—not just for his children, but for the country he led.

CHAPTER THREE

IT WAS too hot to sleep.

The fan above the bed barely moved the still night air, and the fact that Amy had been crying since she put the twins down for the night did not help. Her face was hot and red, so Amy climbed out of bed, opened the French windows and stepped out onto the balcony, wishing for cool night air to hit her cheeks. But in Alzan the nights were warm and, despite a soft breeze, there was no respite.

The desert was lit by a near full moon and Amy looked out across the pale sands in the direction of Alzirz—there, the nights were cold, she had been told. Amy wished that she were there now—not just for the cool of the night, but for other reasons too. In Alzirz a princess could rule.

There girls were not simply dismissed.

But even that didn't ring true. In many ways Alzan was progressive too—there were universities for women, and on Queen Hannah's death the King had ordered that a state-of-the-art maternity hospital be built in her name—not only with the cardiac ward he had mentioned but free obstetric care for all. Sheikh King Emir had pushed his people slowly forward, yet the royals themselves stayed grounded in the ways of old, bound by rules from the past.

The two lands had long ago been one, she had been told—Alzanirz—but they had been separated many generations ago and were now fierce rivals.

She had met King Rakhal and his wife, Natasha, on a few occasions. Natasha was always disarmingly nice and interested in the girls; Rakhal, on the other hand, despite his cool politeness, was guarded. Amy had felt the hatred simmering between the two men, had almost been able to taste the deep rivalry that existed whenever they were both in a room.

Still, it was not the rival King who troubled her tonight, nor was it the King who employed her.

It was her own soul.

She had to leave. She was too involved. Of course she was. Realising the toll her job was taking on her daughter, Amy's mother was urging her to come home. But as Amy stared out to the sands she was conflicted—she simply could not imagine abandoning the twins.

Ummi.

It hurt to hear that word from Clemira and Nakia and to know she would never be one herself.

Amy gulped in air, determined not to start crying again, but though she was dealing with things better these days—though for the most part she had come to terms with her fate—on nights like tonight sometimes the pain surfaced. Sometimes all she could do was mourn a time when happiness had seemed more certain.

Or had it?

She closed her eyes and tried to remember, tried to peer into the dark black hole that was the months and weeks leading up to her accident. Slowly, painfully slowly, she was starting to remember things—choosing her wedding dress, the invitations—but all she could see were images. She simply couldn't recall how she had felt.

Amy had always worked with children, and had been about to marry and start a family of her own when a riding accident had ruined everything. Her hopes and dreams, her relationship and even her fertility had all been taken in one cruel swoop.

Maybe it was for best, Amy pondered—perhaps it was kinder *not* to remember happier times.

It had been a relief to get away from London,

to escape the sympathy and the attention. But Amy's mother had warned her about taking this job—had said it was too much and too soon, that she was running away from her problems. She hadn't been.

The thought of being involved with two babies from birth, of having a very real role in their lives, had been so tempting. Queen Hannah had been well aware of the challenges her daughters would face, and she had told Amy about the disappointment that would sweep the country if her pregnancy produced girls—especially if it proved too dangerous for Hannah to get pregnant again.

Hannah had wanted the girls to be educated in London, to live as ordinary girls there. The plan had been that for four years Amy would take care of the girls in Alzan, but that they would then be schooled in the UK. Amy was to be a huge part of their lives—not a mother, of course, but more than an aunt.

How could she leave now?

How could she walk away because she didn't like the way they were being treated?

Yet how could she stay?

Amy headed down the corridor to do a final check on the twins, her bare feet making no sound. It was a path she trod many times during the day and night, especially now that they were teething. The link from her suite to the twins' sumptuous quarters was a familiar one, but as she entered the room Amy froze—for the sight that greeted her was far from familiar.

There was Emir, his back to her, holding Clemira, who slept on his chest, her head resting on his shoulder, as if it was where she belonged.

Emir stood, silent and strong, and there was a sadness in him that he would surely not want her to witness—a weariness that had only been visible in the first few days after Hannah's death. Then he had gone into *tahir*—had taken himself to the desert for a time of ritual and deep prayer and contemplation. The man who returned to the palace had been different—a remote, aloof man who only occasionally deigned to visit the nursery.

He was far from aloof now as he cradled Clemira. He was wearing black silk lounge pants and nothing else. His top half was bare. Amy had seen him like this before, but then it had not moved her.

In the first dizzy days after the twins had been born they had grappled through the night with two tiny babies. Amy had changed one nappy and handed one fresh, clean baby to Emir, so he could take her to Hannah to feed. Things had been so different then—despite their concern for Hannah there had been love and laughter filling the palace and she missed it so, missed the man she had glimpsed then.

Tonight, for a moment, perhaps that man had returned.

He'd lost weight since then, she noted. His

muscles were now a touch more defined. But there was such tenderness as he held his daughter. It was an intimate glimpse of father and daughter and again she doubted he would want it witnessed. She could sense the aching grief in his wide shoulders—so much so that for a bizarre moment Amy wanted to walk up to him, rest her hand there and offer him silent support. Yet she knew he would not want that, and given she was wearing only her nightdress it was better that she quietly slip away.

'Are you considering leaving?

He turned around just as she was about to go. Amy could not look at him. Normally her head was covered, and her body too—she wondered if she would be chastised tomorrow for being unsuitably dressed—but for now Emir did not appear to notice.

She answered his question as best she could. 'I don't know what to do.'

Clemira stirred in his arms. Gently he placed

her back in her crib and stared down at his daughter for the longest time before turning back to Amy.

'You've been crying.'

'There's an awful lot to cry about.' His black eyes did not reproach her this time. 'I never thought I'd be considering leaving, When Hannah interviewed me—I mean Sheikha Queen—'

'Hannah,' he interrupted. 'That is the name she requested you call her.'

Amy was grateful for the acknowledgement, but she could not speak of this in front of the twins—could not have this conversation without breaking down. So she wished him goodnight and headed back to her room.

'Amy!' he called out to her.

She kept on walking, determined to make it to her room before breaking down, stunned when he followed her through the door.

'You cannot leave Alzan now. I think it would be better for the twins—'

'Of *course* it would be better for the twins to have me stay!' she interrupted, although she should not. Her voice rose again, although it should not. But she was furious. 'Of *course* the twins should have somebody looking after them who loves them—except it's not my job to love them. I'm an employee.'

She watched his eyes shutter for a moment as she hurled back his choice word, but he was right—she *was* an employee, and could be fired at any moment, could be removed from the twins' lives by the flick of his hand. She was thankful for his brutal reminder earlier. She would do well to remember her place.

She brushed past him, trying to get to the safety of the balcony, for it was stifling with him in the room, but before she could get there he halted her.

'You do *not* walk off when I'm talking to you!'

'I do when you're in *my* bedroom!' Amy turned and faced him. 'This happens to be the one place in this prison of a palace where *I* get to make the rules, where I get to speak as I choose, and if you don't like it, if you don't want to hear it, *you* can leave.'

She wanted him out of the room, she wanted him gone, and yet he stepped closer, and it was Amy who stepped back, acutely aware of his maleness, shamefully aware of her own body's conflicted response.

Anger burnt and hissed, but something else did too, for he was an impressive male, supremely beautiful, and of course she had noticed—what woman would not? But down there in his office, or in the safety of the nursery, he was the King and the twins' father, down there he was her boss, but here in this room he was something else.

Somehow she must not show it, so instead she hurled words. 'I *do* love your children, and it's tearing me apart to even think of walking away, but it's been nearly a year since Hannah died and

I can't make excuses any more. If they were my children and you ignored them, then I'd have left you by now. The only difference is I'd have taken them with me...' Her face was red with fury, her blue eyes awash with fresh tears, but there was something more—something she could not tell him. It meant she had to—*had to*—consider leaving, because sometimes when she looked at Emir she wanted the man he had once been to return, and shamefully, guiltily, despite herself, she wanted *him*.

She tore her eyes from his, terrified as to what he might see, and yet he stepped towards her, deliberately stepped towards her. She fought the urge to move towards him—to feel the wrap of his arms around her, for him to shield her from this hell.

It was a hell of his own making, though, Amy remembered, moving away from him and step-ping out onto the balcony, once again ruing the sultry nights.

But it was not just the night that was oppressive. He had joined her outside. She gulped in air, wished the breeze would cool, for it was not just her face that was burning. She felt as if her body was on fire.

'Soon I will marry…' He saw her shoulders tense, watched her hands grip the balcony, and as the breeze caught her nightdress it outlined her shape, detailing soft curves. In that moment Emir could not speak—was this the first time he'd noticed her as a woman?

No.

But this was the first time he allowed himself to properly acknowledge it.

He had seen her in the nursery when he had visited the children a few weeks ago. That day he had sat through a difficult meeting with his elders and advisers, hearing that Queen Natasha was due to give birth soon and being told that soon he must marry.

Emir did not like to be told to do anything, and he rarely ever was.

But in this he was powerless and it did not sit well.

He had walked into the nursery, dark thoughts chasing him. But seeing Amy sitting reading to the twins, her blue eyes looking up, smiling as he entered, he had felt his black thoughts leave him. For the first time in months he had glimpsed peace. Had wanted to stay awhile with his children, with the woman he and Hannah had entrusted to care for them.

He had wanted to hide.

But a king could not hide.

Now what he saw was not so soothing. Now her soft femininity did not bring peace. For a year his passion might as well have been buried in the sands with his wife. For a year he had not fought temptation—there had been none. But something had changed since that moment in the nursery, since that day when he had noticed not just her smile but her mouth, not just her words but her voice. At first those thoughts had been stealthy, invading dreams over which he had no control, but now they were bolder and crept in by day. The scent of her perfume in an empty corridor might suddenly reach him, telling him the path she had recently walked, reminding him of a buried dream. And the mention of her name when she had requested a meeting had hauled him from loftier thoughts to ones more basic.

And basic were his thoughts now, yet he fought them.

He tried to look at the problem, not the temptation before him, the woman standing with her back to him. He wanted to turn her around, wanted to in a way he hadn't in a long time. But he was not locked in dreams now. He had control here and he forced himself to speak on.

'I did look through your contract and you are right. It has not been adhered to.'

Still she did not turn to look at him, though her

body told her to. She wished he would leave— could not deal with him here even if it was to discuss the twins.

'After their birthday things are going to get busy here,' Emir said.

'When you select your bride and marry?'

He did not answer directly. 'These are complicated times for Alzan. Perhaps it would be better if the girls spent some time in London— a holiday.'

She closed her eyes, knew what was coming. Yes, a flight on his luxury jet, a few weeks at home with the twins, time with her family, luxurious hotels… What was there to say no to? Except… She took a deep breath and turned to him. 'Without you?'

'Yes,' Emir said.

She looked at the man who had so loved his children, who was now so closed off, so remote, so able to turn from them, and she had to know why.

'Is it because they remind you of Hannah?' Amy asked. 'Is that why it hurts so much to have them around?'

'Leave it,' he said. He wished the answer was that simple, wished there was someone in whom he could confide. 'I will have the trip scheduled.'

'So you can remove them a bit more from your life?'

'You do *not* talk to me like that.'

'Here I do.'

'Once I am married the twins will have a mother figure…'

'Oh, please!'

He frowned at her inappropriate response, but that did not deter her.

'Is it a mother for the twins you are selecting or a bride to give you sons?'

'I've told you already: it is not for you to question our ways. What would you know…?'

'Plenty.' Amy retorted. 'My parents divorced when I was two and I remember going to my father's; I remember when he married his new wife—a woman who had no interest in his children, who would really have preferred that we didn't inconvenience her one Saturday in two.' She stopped her tirade. There was no point. This was about the twins, not her past.

But instead of telling her off again, instead of telling her her words were inappropriate, he asked questions.

'How did you deal with it as a child?' Emir asked—because it mattered. He did want to make things better for his girls. 'Were you unhappy? Were you…?'

'Ignored?' She finished his sentence for him and Emir nodded, making her tell him some of her truth. 'Dad bought me a dolls' house.' She gave a pale smile at the memory. 'I spent hours playing with it. There the mum and dad slept and ate together. The kids played in the garden or in the living room, not up in their room…' There she'd been able to fix things. Her smile faded and trembled. Here she couldn't fix things.

She felt his hand on her bare arm, felt his fingers brush her skin as if to comfort.

It did not.

She felt his flesh meet hers and it was all she could think of. His dark hand making contact was *all* she could think of when her mind should surely be only on the twins.

She hauled her thoughts back to them. 'Can I ask,' she said, 'that when you consider a bride you think of them?'

'Of course.'

His voice was soft and low, his hand still warm on her arm and there was a different tension surrounding them, the certainty that she was but a second away from a kiss.

A kiss that could only spell danger.

Perhaps that was his plan? Amy thought, shrugging off his hand, turning again to the desert. Perhaps he wanted her to fall in love with him. How convenient to keep her here, to bind her a little closer to the twins, to ensure that she did not resign. For he deemed her *better* for the twins.

'Leave!' She spat the word out over her shoulder, but still he stood. 'Leave…' she said again. But there was no relief when he complied, no respite when she heard the door close. Amy choked back angry tears as she stood on the balcony, she wanted to call him back, wanted to continue their discussion….wanted…

There was the other reason she had to consider leaving.

Despite herself, despite the way he had been these past months, when he made any brief appearance in the nursery, on the rare occasions when he deigned to appear, her heart foolishly leapt at the sight of him—and lately her dreams had allowed more intimate glimpses of him. It confused her that she could have feelings for a man who paid so little attention to his own children.

Feelings that were forbidden.

Hidden.

And they must stay that way, Amy told herself, climbing into bed and willing sleep to come. But she was nervous all the same, for when she woke it would be morning.

And tomorrow she would be alone in the desert with him.

CHAPTER FOUR

'COME in.'

Amy's smile wasn't returned as the bedroom door opened and Fatima walked in.

'I'm nearly ready.'

'What are you doing?' Fatima frowned, her serious eyes moving over the mountain of coloured paper scattered over Amy's bed.

'I'm just wrapping some presents to take for the twins. I hadn't had a chance before.' She hadn't had a chance because after a night spent tossing and turning, wondering if she'd misread things, wondering what might have happened had she not told Emir to leave, Amy had, for the first time since she'd taken the role as nanny, overslept.

Normally she was up before the twins, but

this morning it had been their chatter over the intercom that had awoken her and now, having given them breakfast and got them bathed and dressed, five minutes before their departure for the desert, she had popped them in their cots so she could quickly wrap the gifts.

'Their time in the desert is to be solemn,' Fatima said.

'It's their birthday.'

'The celebrations will be here at the palace.' She stood and waited as Amy removed the gifts from her open case. 'The King is ready to leave now. I will help you board the helicopter with the twins.' She called to another servant to collect Amy's case.

'You need to take the twins' cases also,' Amy told him.

'I have taken care of that.' Fatima clearly did not want the King to be kept waiting. 'Come now.'

Perhaps she had imagined last night, for Emir

barely glanced at the twins and was his usual dismissive self with Amy as they boarded the helicopter. Amy was grateful for Fatima's help to strap the twins in. The twins were used to flying, and so too was Amy, but what was different this time was the lack of aides—usually at the very least Patel travelled with them, but this trip, as she had been told many times, would be different.

Amy could almost forgive his silence and his lack of interaction with the girls during the flight, for she was well aware that this was a journey he should have been making with his wife. Perhaps he was more pensive than dismissive?

Emir was more than pensive: he looked out to the desert with loathing, and the sun glinting on the canyons made him frown as he stared into the distance. He remembered the rebels who'd used to reside there—men who had refused to wait for the predictions to come true, who'd wanted Alzan to be gone and had taken matters into their own bloody hands.

'It's beautiful,' Amy commented as they swept deeper into the desert. She'd said it more to herself, but Emir responded.

'From a distance,' Emir said. 'But the closer you get…'

He did not finish. Instead he went back to staring broodily out of the window, replaying battles of the past in his mind, hearing the pounding hooves and the cries, feeling the grit of sand rubbed in wounds, history in every grain. Yet above all that he could hear *her*, reading a book to the twins, hear his daughters laughing as they impatiently turned the pages. He wanted to turn to the sound of them, to forget the pain and suffering, to set aside the past, but as King he had sworn to remember.

The heat hit Amy as soon as she stepped out of the helicopter. Emir held Nakia, while Amy carried Clemira and even though the helicopter had landed as close as possible to the compound of tents still the walk was hard work—the shifting soft sand made each step an effort. Once inside a tent, she took off her shoes and changed into slippers as Emir instructed. She thanked the pilot, who had brought in her suitcase, and then Emir led her through a passageway and after that another, as he briefly explained what would happen.

'The girls will rest before we take them to the Bedouins. There is a room for you next to them.'

They were in what appeared to be a lounge, its sandy floor hidden beneath layer after layer of the most exquisite rugs. The different areas were all separated by coloured drapes. It was like being in the heart of a vibrant labyrinth and already she felt lost.

'There are refreshments through there,' Emir explained, 'but the twins are not to have any. Today they must eat and drink only from the desert...'

Amy had stopped listening. She spun around as she heard the sound of the helicopter taking off. 'He's forgotten to bring in their luggage!' She went to run outside, but she took a wrong turn and ran back into the lounge again, appalled that Emir wasn't helping. 'You have to stop him—we need to get the twins' bags.'

'They do not need the things you packed for them. They are here to learn the ways of the desert and to be immersed in them. Everything they need is here.'

'I didn't just pack toys for them!' She could hear the noise of the chopper fading in the distance. Well, he'd just have to summon someone to get it turned around. 'Emir—I mean, Your Highness.' Immediately Amy corrected herself, for she had addressed him as she had so long ago. 'It's not toys or fancy clothes that I'm worried about. It's their bottles, their formula.'

'Here they will drink water from a cup,' Emir said.

'You can't do that to them!' Amy could not believe what she was hearing. 'That's far too harsh.'

'Harsh?' Emir interrupted. 'This land is harsh. This land is brutal and unforgiving. Yet its people have learnt to survive in it. When you are royal, when your life is one of privilege, it is expected that at least once a year you are true to the desert.'

Where, she wondered, had the caring father gone? Where was the man who had rocked his tiny babies in strong arms? Who even last night had picked up his sleeping child just to hold her? Maybe she really had dreamt it—maybe she had imagined last night—for he stood now unmoved as Clemira and Nakia picked up on the tension and started to cry.

'We will leave soon,' Emir said.

'It's time for their nap now,' Amy said. She was expecting another argument, but instead he nodded.

'When they wake we will leave.'

'Is there anyone to help? To show me where they rest? Where the kitchen…?'

'It's just us.'

'Just us?' Amy blinked.

'There is a groundsman to tend to the animals, but here in the tent and out in the desert we will take care of ourselves.'

Oh, she had known they would be alone in the desert, but she had thought he had meant alone by royal standards—she had been quite sure that there would be servants and maidens to help them. Not once had she imagined that it would truly be just them, and for the first time the vastness and the isolation of the desert scared her.

'What if something happens?' Amy asked. 'What if one of the girls gets ill?'

'The Bedouins trust me to make the right decisions for their land and for their survival. It is right that in turn I trust them.'

'With your children?'

'Again,' Emir said, 'I have to warn you not to question our ways. Again,' he stated, 'I have to remind you that you are an employee.'

Her cheeks burned in anger but Amy scooped up the twins and found their resting area. Maybe he was right, she thought with a black smile. Maybe *she* needed time in the desert, for she was too used to things being done for her—a bit too used to having things unpacked and put away. And, yes, she was used to ringing down to the palace kitchen to have bottles warmed and food prepared. Now she had to settle two hungry, frazzled babies in the most unfamiliar surroundings.

The wind made the tent walls billow, and the low wooden cribs that lay on the floor were nothing like what the twins were used to—neither were the cloth nappies she changed them into. Emir came in with two cups of water for the girls, but that just upset them more, and when he'd left Amy took ages rocking the cribs to get the twins to settle. Her anger towards Emir rose as she did so, and it was a less than impressed Amy who finally walked out to the sight of Emir resting on the cushions.

He looked at her tightly pressed lips, saw the anger burning in her cheeks as she walked past him, and offered a rare explanation. 'There are traditions that must be upheld. Sit.' Emir watched her fingers clench at his command and perhaps wisely rephrased it. 'Please be seated. I will explain what is to take place.'

It was awkward to sit on the low cushions, but Amy remembered to tuck her feet away from him. It was difficult facing him again after last night—not that he appeared to remember it, for his eyes did not even search her face. Really he seemed rather bored at having to explain things.

'I understand that you think this is cruel, but really it is not...'

'I never said cruel,' Amy corrected. 'I said it was harsh on the girls. Had you told me earlier what was to happen I could have better prepared them. I could have had them drinking from cups.'

He conceded with a nod, and now he did look at her—could see not just the anger but that she was upset, and on behalf of his children. 'I know the year has been a difficult one. I am grateful the girls have had you.'

She was disarmed by his sudden niceness, forgot to thank him as she ought to, but Emir did not seem to notice. 'I have not been looking forward to this. Which is why, perhaps, I did not explain things. I have been trying not to think about it. Hannah was not looking forward to this time either.' Amy blinked at the revelation. 'Hannah wanted it left till the last moment— till they were a little older. I was trying to follow her wish, I did not think about cups…' He gave a shrug.

'Of course not,' Amy conceded. 'I don't expect

you to. But if there was just more communication it might make things easier.'

'If she were alive still this would be difficult.'

Amy could see the battle in his face to keep his features bland, almost hear the effort to keep sentiment from his voice.

'If she were here Hannah would not have been able to feed them, and that would have upset her.' Amy frowned as he continued. 'This is a time when babies are…' He did not know the word. 'Separated from their mother's milk.'

'Weaned off it?'

Emir nodded. 'Tradition states that they should travel for a week living on water and fruits. The desert people do not approve that I am only giving them the girls for one night, and King Rakhal also opposed it, but I explained that my children have already been…' he paused before he used the word that was new to his vocabulary '…weaned at two weeks of age.'

'And he agreed to reduce it?'

'Not for my daughters' sake.' Emir's voice deepened in hate. 'Only, I believe, because his wife is pregnant. Only because I reminded him that the rule would apply to his infant too.' He gave a rare smile. 'Perhaps Queen Natasha found out about it.'

Amy smiled back. She looked at him and was curious—more curious than she had ever been about a man. There was just so much about him she did not know, so much she had wrongly assumed. These past weeks it had not been bottles and cups on his mind, it had been their welfare. That this proud King had gone to his enemy to ask a favour spoke volumes, but it just confused her more.

'Natasha is English, like you.' Emir broke into her thoughts. 'And would be just as opposed, I presume.' His smile was wry now. 'Poor Rakhal!'

'Poor Natasha,' was Amy's response. 'If Rakhal is as stubborn as you.'

He told her some more about what would happen—that they would set off soon and would take lunch at the oasis. 'It must be soon,' Emir said, 'for the winds are gathering and we have to make it to the oasis today, so all this can take place before their first birthday.'

He did have their best interests at heart, Amy realised, even if he did not always show it. At every turn he confused her, for when the twins woke from that nap it was Emir who went to them, who helped her wrap them in shawls. When she saw him smile down at Clemira as they headed outside he was like the Emir she had once seen.

As they turned to the right of the tent Amy felt her heart sink at the familiar sound of horses whinnying—it was a sound that had once been pleasing to her, but now it only brought terror.

'Horses?' She looked at the beasts. 'We're riding to the oasis?'

'Of course.' He handed her Clemira, oblivious to the panic in her voice.

'Your Highness…'

'Emir,' he conceded.

'Emir—I can't. I thought we'd be driving.'

'Driving?' He shot out an incredulous laugh. 'You really have no idea what this is about.'

'I honestly don't think I can ride,' Amy said.

'Walk, then.' Emir shrugged. 'Though I suggest you walk alongside a horse, for it will only be a short time before you surely decide you're not so precious.'

'It's not that!' He was so arrogant, so difficult to speak to at times. She certainly wasn't going to tell him about her accident. She didn't want a lecture on how it was better to get back on a horse, or some withering comment, or—worse—questions. 'I'm nervous around horses,' she offered.

Emir just shrugged. 'I will travel alone, then,' he said. 'You will help me to secure the twins.'

Amy bristled. He certainly wasn't going to baby her—after all, he didn't even pander to the twins. She wondered if they would fight and struggle as she secured them, but instead the girls were delighted with this new game—giggling as he balanced each one against his chest. It was Amy who was struggling as she wrapped a sash over his shoulder and tied a knot low on his waist, for she had never been closer to him.

'That's Clemira.' She did her best to keep her voice light, hoped he would not notice her shaking fingers as she wrapped the second twin and was glad to walk around to his back so he would not see her blush. She lifted his *kafeya* a little, ran the cloth behind it. Her fingers paused as she felt dark skin. She bit on her lip as she saw the nape of his neck, resisting the urge to linger.

'Done?' he asked.

'Nearly.' She finished the knot on his shoulder. 'Are you sure you can manage them both?'

'I have carried much more.' He indicated to Raul, the groundsman, to bring over his horse. As he mounted with ease the twins started to get upset—perhaps realising that they were leaving Amy behind.

'They will be fine,' Emir said.

But wasn't it *her* job to make this transition easier for them? As painful as it would be, she wanted to be there for the girls when they were handed over to strangers—wanted this last bit of time with them.

'I'll come.' The words tumbled out. 'It will be better for the girls if I ride along beside them and give them their lunch.'

'It is up to you.' Emir's voice did not betray the fact that he was relieved. He had privately been wondering how he would manage—not the ride, but the time at the oasis.

When he saw her tentativeness as she approached her animal, saw that her fear was real, he halted their departure for a moment and called to Raul, translating for Amy. 'I have asked him to bring Layyinah. She is, as her name attests, the most gentle mare.'

Layyinah was gorgeous—white and elegant, and more beautiful than any horse Amy had seen. She had huge eyes and nostrils, her forehead was broad, and Amy ran a hand over a magnificent mane.

'She's beautiful,' Amy said. 'I mean *seriously* beautiful.'

'Pure Arabian,' Emir explained. 'That bulge between her eyes is her *jibbah*. There is more...' he did not know the word '...more room that helps with her breathing in the hot air. They are built for this land. In our horses we put a lot of trust and they return it. She will look after you.'

Amy actually wanted to get on, although she was incredibly nervous. The once familiar action took her a couple of attempts, and though her robes had enough cloth in them to allow for decency it felt strange to be climbing onto a horse wearing them. But Emir had managed, Amy told herself. As she took to the saddle she was glad he had mounted his horse first, because he was there beside her, surprisingly patient and encouraging, as she took a moment to settle. The horse moved a few steps as it became accustomed to a new rider.

'*Kef.*' Emir leant over and pulled at the rein. 'It means stop,' he explained, and waited till Amy had her breath back. 'How does it feel?'

'Good,' Amy admitted. 'It feels scary, but good.'

'We will take it slowly,' Emir said. 'There is nothing to be nervous about.'

Oh, there was—but she chose not to tell him.

As they set off, even though it felt different riding on sand, the motion was soon familiar, and Amy realised how much she had missed riding. It had been a huge part of her life but she had never considered resuming it. Had never envisiaged the day she would be brave enough to try again—unexpectedly, that day was here.

She breathed in the warm air, felt the beauty of her surrounds, and for the first time she put anger and her questions aside, just drank in the moment. She heard Emir talk to his children, heard their chatter and laughter as they set off on an adventure. It was nicer just to enjoy rather than think about where this journey would take them.

'It's gorgeous.'

Emir merely shrugged.

'So peaceful.'

'When she chooses to be,' came Emir's strange answer, and he looked over to her. 'Don't let the desert seduce you. As my father told me, she is like a beautiful woman: she dazzles and lulls you, but she is always plotting.'

'What happened to your father?'

'He was killed.' Emir pointed to the distance. 'Over there.'

Despite the heat she shivered. 'And your mother?'

He did not answer.

'Emir?'

'It is not a tale to be told on your first night in the desert.' He changed the subject. 'Soon we will be there.' He pointed ahead to a shimmer on the horizon. 'Do you see the shadows?'

'Not really,' Amy admitted, but as they rode on she started to see the shadows that were in fact huge trees and shrubs.

'What will happen?'

'We will select our lunch,' Emir said, 'and then we will wait for the desert people.' He looked over, saw her tense profile, and then he looked down at the twins, lulled by the motion of the horse, safe with their father. They had both fallen asleep and he did not want to hand them over either—hating so many of his kingdom's ways.

'They've missed you.'

He heard Amy's voice but did not respond, for he had missed then so much too, and he could not share with her the reasons why.

Or perhaps he could.

He looked over as, bolder now, she rode ahead

of him, her eyes on the oasis. Her scarf kept slipping, her hair was blowing behind her, and the attraction he felt was acknowledged. What just a couple of generations ago would have been forbidden was a possibility now. After all, Rakhal had an English wife—maybe there could be a way…

Poor Rakhal?

Perhaps not.

Poor Natasha. Even if they had been said as a light joke, he recalled Amy's words, knew from their conversation she was not one who would be told what to do. She would not meekly comply to his request or be flattered that he'd asked.

She was trotting now, and Emir frowned. For someone so nervous around horses, someone who hadn't wanted to ride, she was doing incredibly well. She looked as if she had been riding for years. He had a glimpse then of a different future—riding through the Alzan desert alongside her, with Clemira and Nakia and their own children too.

He must not rush this decision—and he certainly must not rush *her*.

She pulled up her horse and turned and smiled then, her face flushed from the exertion, her eyes for once unguarded, exhilarated. Emir wanted to see more of that and, patience forgotten, kicked his horse faster to join her, his urgency building with each gallop. He wanted her wild and free in his bed. Today—tonight—he would convince her. And as he slowed to a walk beside her, as he saw the spread of colour on her cheeks darken as he looked over to her, as he registered she wanted him too, he thanked the desert that had brought him a simple solution.

Maybe his kingdom and his family could somehow remain.

CHAPTER FIVE

'*LA,*' Emir scolded, frowning as Nakia spat out the fruit he'd tried to feed her. 'I mean *no*!' He was fast realising that the twins mainly understood English. 'She copies her sister.'

Amy couldn't help but laugh. They were deep in the desert, sitting by the oasis, feeding the children fresh fruit that they had collected from the lush trees—or they were *trying* to feed the children, because a moment ago Clemira had done the same thing, spitting out the fruit and screwing up her face.

'Clemira is the leader.' Amy watched his jaw tighten. It would seem she had said yet another thing of which he did not approve.

Their time at the oasis was not exactly turning out to be a stunning success. As soon as Emir had put her down Clemira had promptly tried to eat the sand, and Nakia had copied and got some in her eyes.

These were two thoroughly modern princesses, thanks to Amy. They were more used to bopping around to a DVD she'd had sent from home, or swimming in the impressive palace pool, than sitting by an oasis waiting for some elder from the Bedouins to come and offer wisdom for the life journey ahead of them.

'They know nothing of our ways,' Emir said, and though Amy was tempted to murmur that she wondered why that was, she bit her tongue. 'Hannah was worried about this. She didn't like the idea of them fasting.'

'It's not fasting.' Amy was practical; she understood now why he had put this off. 'If they're hungry, they'll eat. They have finally started to drink water.'

'They are spoilt,' Emir said as Clemira again spat out the fruit he offered.

'I know,' Amy admitted. 'And it's completely my fault—I can't help it.'

To her utter surprise, he laughed. She hadn't heard him laugh in a very long while. Even though the twins were being naughty, since they had arrived at the oasis Emir had been different. He seemed more relaxed—like a father to the twins, even—and then she looked up and saw he was watching her. She blushed a little as she looked back, for he was still looking at her.

She had no idea she was being seduced, no idea that the man lounging beside her, relaxed and calm, nurtured serious intentions.

'I was not criticising you,' Emir said. 'I am glad that you spoil them. You are right—I should have given you more notice. Perhaps you could have prepared them.'

'Now I've thought about it, I don't know how I could have,' Amy admitted. 'They're going to be terrified when the Bedouin take them.'

'They are kind people,' Emir said. 'They will do them no harm.'

But his heart wasn't in it. He tasted again the fear he had felt when he was a child—could remember his screams as the wizened old man took him. He hated the rules that bound him.

Hated Rakhal.

It was kinder to his soul to look at Amy, to visit another possible option.

'What happens tomorrow when we get back to the palace?' Amy asked, unnerved by his scrutiny and desperately trying to think of something to say. 'Will it be very grand?'

'There will be a party. My brother Hassan, the second in line, should attend.'

'Should?'

'He has a great interest in horses too...' Emir gave a wry smile. 'They take up a lot of his time.'

She had heard about Prince Hassan and his wild ways, though she had never met him, just heard the whispers.Of course some things were never discussed, so she stayed silent.

She was surprised when Emir said more. 'Though his interest in horses is something I do not condone.'

She gave a small shocked laugh at his admission.

'He needs to grow up,' Emir said.

'Maybe he's happier not.'

'Perhaps,' he admitted, and thought perhaps now he understood his brother a little.

He had confronted him many times, to no avail. Emir did not get the thrill his brother found in winning—did not understand why Hassan would roam the globe from casino to casino. Hassan had everything and more a man needed right here in Alzan. Riches aplenty, and any woman of his choosing.

He looked over to Amy. One of her hands was idly patting the sand into a mound. For the first time with a woman Emir was not certain of the outcome, but he glimpsed the thrill of the chase, the anticipation before victory.

He understood Hassan a little better now.

'King Rakhal will also be attending.'

'With his wife?' Amy checked. She had briefly met Natasha, but she remembered who she was speaking about. 'I meant will Queen Natasha be attending?'

'No.' Emir shook his head. 'She is due to give birth soon, so it is safer that she does not travel. She seems very happy here,' he pushed gently. 'At first I am sure it was daunting, but she seems to have taken well to her new role.'

'Can I ask something?' Emir was still looking at her, still inviting conversation.

Her question was not the one he was hoping for: it did not appear as if she was envisaging herself for a moment as Queen.

'Why, if their baby is a girl, can she rule?'

'Their laws are different,' Emir said. 'Do you

know that Alzan and Alzirz were once the same country?'

'Alzanirz?' Amy nodded.

'There have always been twins in our royal lineage,' Emir explained. 'Many generations ago a ruler of the time had twin sons. They were unexpected, and were not branded, so the people were unsure who the rightful heir was. It was a troubled time for the country and the King sought a solution. It was decided that the land would be divided, that each son would rule his own kingdom. The predictors of the time said that one day they would reunite...but we were both given separate rules. As soon as one rule is broken the country must become one again, the ruler being of the lineage which survived.'

'It doesn't seem fair.' She looked to his dark eyes and blinked, for they were not stern, and instead of chastising her he nodded for her to go on. 'If a princess can rule there, why not here?'

'They have another rule that they must abide

by,' Emir explained. 'In Alzirz the ruler can marry only once. Rakhal's mother died in childbirth and he was not expected to survive—the prophecy was almost fulfilled.'

'But he survived?'

Emir nodded. 'Here...' He was silent for a moment before continuing. 'Here the law states that if the ruler's partner dies he can marry again.' Still he looked into her eyes. 'As must I.'

'Must?'

'The people are unsettled—especially with an impending birth in Alzirz.'

'But if you are not ready...' Amy bit her tongue, knew that to discuss would be pointless.

'Ready?' He frowned, for who was she to question him? But then he remembered she came from a land that relied on the fickle formula of attraction. The glimmer of his idea glowed brighter still. The answer to his dilemma sat beside him now, and her voice, Emir noticed, was just a little breathy when she spoke to him.

'Perhaps a year is too soon to expect...' She licked dry lips, wished she could suddenly be busy with the twins, for this conversation was far too intimate, but the girls were sitting playing with each other. 'Marriage is a huge step.'

'And a step I must take seriously. Though...' He must not rush her, Emir was aware of that. 'I am not thinking of marriage today.'

'Oh...'

Sometimes he made her dizzy. Sometimes when he looked at her with those black eyes it was all she could do to return his gaze. Sometimes she was terrified he would see the lust that burnt inside her.

Not all the time.

But at times.

And this was one of them.

Sometimes, and this was also one of them, she held the impossible thought that he might kiss her—that the noble head might lower a fraction to hers. The sun must be making her crazy because she could almost taste his mouth… The conversation *was* too intimate.

His next words made her burn.

'You are worried about tonight?' Emir said. 'About what might happen?' He saw the dart of her eyes, saw her top teeth move to her lower lip. He could kiss her mouth *now*, could feel her want, was almost certain of it. He would confirm it now. 'They will be fine.'

'They?'

Her eyes narrowed as his words confused her and he knew then that in her mind she had been alone in the tent with him. Emir suppressed a triumphant smile.

'They will be looked after,' he assured her. And so too, Emir decided, would she.

Embarrassed, she turned away, looked to the oasis, to the clear cool water. She wished she could jump in, for her cheeks were on fire now and she was honest enough with herself to know why. Perhaps it was she who was not ready for the presence of a new sheikha queen?

How foolish had she been to think he might have been about to kiss her? That Emir might even see her in that way?

'I have thought about what you said—about the girls needing someone…' He should be patient and yet he could not. 'You love my daughters.'

He said it as a fact.

It *was* a fact.

She stared deeper into the water, wondered if she was crazy with the thoughts she was entertaining—that Emir might be considering her as his lover, a mistress, a proxy mother for his girls. Then she felt his hand on her cheek and she could not breathe. She felt his finger trace down to her throat and caress the piece of flesh she truly loathed.

'What is this from?' His strong fingers were surprisingly gentle, his skin cool against her warm throat, and his questions, his touch, were both gentle and probing.

'Please, Emir…'

The Bedouin caravan was travelling towards them, the moment they were both dreading nearing. A kiss would have to wait. He stood and watched them approach—a line of camels and their riders. He listened to his daughters laughing, knowing in a short while there would be the sound of tears, and he wanted to bury his head in Amy's hair. He wanted the escape of her mouth. And yet now there was duty.

He stood and picked up both daughters, looked into their eyes so dark and trusting. He could not stand to hand them over, for he remembered being ripped from his own parents' arms, his own screams and pleas, and then the campfire and the strange faces and he remembered his own fear. Right now he hated the land that he ruled—hated the ways of old and the laws that could not be changed without both Kings' agreement.

He had survived it, Emir told himself as the wizened old man approached. The twins shrieked in terror as he held out his arms to them.

Emir walked over and spoke with the man, though Amy could not understand what was said.

'They are upset—you need to be kind with them,' Emir explained.

'It is your fear that scares them.' The black eyes were young in his wizened old face. 'You do not wish to come and speak with me?'

'I have decisions I must make alone.'

'Then make them!' the old man said.

'They are difficult ones.'

'Difficult if made from the palace, perhaps,' the old man said. 'But here the only king is the desert—it always brings solutions if you ask for them.'

Emir walked back to Amy, who should be standing in silence as the old man prepared the sand. But of course she was not.

'Who is he?' Amy asked.

'He's an elder of the Bedouins,' Emir explained. 'He is supposed to be more than one hundred and twenty years old.'

'That's impossible.'

'Not out here,' Emir said, without looking over. 'He gives wisdom to those who choose to ask for it.'

'Do *you*?' Amy asked, and then stammered an apology, for it was not her place to ask such things.

But Emir deigned a response. 'I have consulted him a few times,' he admitted, 'but not lately.' He gave a shrug. 'His answers are never straightforward...'

The old man filled two small vials with the sand he had blessed and Emir knew what was to come.

Amy felt her heart squeezing as he took the sobbing babies, and her pain turned to horror as he walked with them towards the water.

'What's happening?'

'They are to be immersed in the water and then they will be taken to the camp.'

'Emir—*no!*'

'You have rituals for your babies, do you not?' Emir snapped. 'Do babies in England not cry?'

He was right, but in that moment Amy felt as if she were bleeding, hearing their shrieks and not having the chance to kiss them goodbye. Listening to them sob as they were taken, she was not just upset; she was furious too—with herself for the part she was playing in this and with Emir.

'Ummi!' both twins screamed in the distance, and worse than her fear of his anger was resisting her urge to run to them. 'Ummi!'

She heard the fading cry and then she heard her own ones—stood there and sobbed. She didn't care if he was angry about what they called her. Right now she just ached for the babies.

And as he stood watching her weep for his children, as he heard them cry out for her, Emir knew his decision was the right one.

'They will be okay,' he tried to comfort her. 'These are the rules.'

'I thought kings made the rules,' she retorted angrily.

'This is the way of our land.' He should be angry, should reprimand her, silence her, but instead he sought to comfort her. 'They will be taken care of. They will be sung to and taught their history.' His hand was on her cheek. 'And each year that passes they will understand more...'

'I can't do this again.' So upset was Amy she did not focus on his touch, just on the thought of next year and the next, of watching the babies she loved lost to strange laws. 'I can't do this, Emir,' she was frantic. 'I have to leave.'

'No,' Emir said, for he could not lose her now. 'You can be here for them—comfort them and explain to them.'

She could. He knew that. The answer to his prayers was here and he bent his mouth and tasted her, tasted the salty tears on her cheeks, and then his lips moved to her mouth and her fear for the girls was replaced, but only with terror.

She was kissing a king. And she *was* kissing him. Her mouth was seeking an escape from her agony and for a moment she found it. She let her mind hush to the skill of his lips and his arms wrapped around her, drew her closer to him. His tongue did not prise open her lips because they opened readily, and she knew where this was leading—knew the plans he had in mind.

He wanted her to be here for his daughters—wanted to ensure she would stay. She pulled back, as her head told her to, because for Amy this was a dangerous game. With this kiss came her heart.

'*No.*' She wanted to get away, wanted this moment never to have happened. She could not be his lover—especially when soon he would take a bride. 'We can't…'

'We *can*.' He was insistent. His lips found hers again and her second taste was her downfall, for it made her suddenly weak.

His hands were on her hips and he pulled her firmly in, his mouth making clear his intent, and she had never felt more wanted, more feminine. His passion was her pleasure, his desire was what she had been missing, but she could not be his plaything, could not confuse things further.

'Emir, no.'

'*Yes.*' He could see it so clearly now—wondered why it had taken so long. 'We go now to the tent and make love.'

Again he kissed her. His mind had been busy

seeking a solution, but it stilled when he tasted her lips. The pleasure he had forgone was now remembered, except with a different slant—for he tasted not any woman, but Amy. And she was more than simply pleasing. He liked the stilling of her breath as his mouth shocked her, liked the fight for control beneath his hands. Her mouth was still but her body was succumbing; he felt her momentary pause and then her mouth gave in to him, and for Emir there was something un-expected—an emotion he had never tasted in a woman. All the anger she had held in check was delivered in her response. It was a savage kiss that met him now, a different kiss, and he was hard in response. The gentle lovemaking he had intended, the tender seduction he had pictured, changed as she kissed him back.

He was surprised by the intensity of her pas-sion, by the bundle of emotion in his arms, for though she fought him still her mouth was kiss-ing him.

It was Emir who withdrew. He looked down at her flushed, angry face.

'Why the temper, Amy?'

'Because I didn't want you to *know*!'

'Know?' And he looked down and saw the lust she had kept hidden, felt the burn of her arousal beneath him. It consumed him, endeared her to him, told him his decision was the right one. 'Why would you not want me to know?'

'Because...' His mouth was at her ear, his breath making her shiver. She turned her face away at the admission, but it did not stop his pursuit, more stealthy now, and more delicious. 'It can come to nothing.'

'It can...' Emir said. She loathed her own weakness, but now she had tasted him she wanted him so.

'Please...' The word spilled from her lips; it sounded as if she was begging. 'Take me back to the tent.'

Except he wanted her *now*. His hands were

at the buttons of her robe, pulling it down over her shoulders. Their kisses were frantic, their want building. She grappled with his robe, felt the leather that held his sword and the power of the man who was about to make love to her. She was kissing a king and it terrified her, but still it was delicious, still it inflamed her as his words attempted to soothe her.

'The people will come to accept it…'

He was kissing her neck now, moving down to her exposed breast. She ached for his mouth there, ached to give in to his mastery, but her mind struggled to understand his words. 'The people…?'

'When I take you as my bride.'

'Bride!' He might as well have pushed her into the water. She felt the plunge into confusion and struggled to come up for air, felt the horror as history repeated itself. It was happening again.

'Emir—no!'

'*Yes.*' He thought she was overwhelmed by

his offer—did not recognise she was dying in his arms, as his mouth moved back to take her again, to calm her. But when she spoke he froze.

'I can't have children.'

She watched the words paralyse him, saw his pupils constrict, and then watched him make an attempt to right his features. To his credit he did not drop her, but his arms stilled at her sides and then his forehead rested on hers as the enormity of her words set in.

'I had a riding accident and it left me unable to have children.' Somehow she managed to speak; somehow, before she broke down, she managed to find her voice.

'I'm sorry.'

'My fiancé was too.'

With a sob she turned from him, pulled her robe over her naked breasts and did up the buttons as she ran to where the horses were tethered. She didn't possess any fear as she untied her mare and mounted it, because fear was nothing compared to grief. She kicked her into a canter and when that did not help she galloped. She could hear the sound of Emir's beast rapidly gaining on her, could hear his shouts for her to halt, and finally she did, turning her pained eyes to him.

'I lay for five days on a machine that made me breathe and I heard my fiancé speaking with his mother. That was how I found out I couldn't have children. That was how I heard him say there really was no point marrying me…' She was breathless from riding, from anger, yet still she shouted. 'Of course that's not what he told me when I came round—he said the accident had made him realise that, though he cared, he didn't love me, that life was too short and he wasn't ready for commitment.' Emir said nothing. 'But I knew the reason he really left.'

'He's a fool, then.'

'So what does that make you?'

'I am King,' Emir answered, and it was the only answer he could give.

As soon as the tent was in sight, it was Emir who kicked his horse on, Emir who raced through the desert, and she was grateful to be left alone, to gallop, to sob, to think…

To remember.

The black hole of the accident was filling painfully—each stride from Layyinah was taking her back there again. She was a troubled bride-to-be, a young woman wondering if she wasn't making the most appalling mistake. The sand and the dunes changed to countryside; she could hear hooves pounding mud and feel the cool of spring as she came to an appalling conclusion.

She had to call the wedding off.

CHAPTER SIX

'I HAVE run you a bath.'

Emir looked up as Amy walked into the tent. He had told Raul to watch her from a distance and, after showering, had run the first bath of his life.

And it was for another.

As he had done so his gut had churned with loathing towards her fiancé—loathing that was immediately reflected in a mirror that shone back to him, for wasn't he now doing the same?

Yet he was a king.

Again that thought brought no solace.

'Thank you.'

Her pale smile as she walked into the tent confused him. He had expected anger, bitterness to enter the tent with her, but if anything she seemed calm.

Amy *was* calm.

Calmer than she had been since the accident.

She unzipped her robe and looked around the bathing area. It was lit by candles in hurricane jars—not, she realised, a romantic gesture from Emir, it was how the whole tent was lit. Yet she was touched all the same.

Amy slid into the fragrant water and closed her eyes, trying and failing not to think of the twins and how they would be coping. Doing her best not to think of Emir and what he had proposed.

Instead she looked at her past—at a time she could now clearly remember. It felt good to have it back.

She washed her hair and climbed out of the water, drying herself with the towel and then wrapping it around her. Aware she was dressed rather inappropriately, she hoped Emir would be in his sleeping area, but he was sitting on cushions as she walked quietly past him, heading to her sleeping area to put on something rather more suitable, before she faced a conversation with him.

He looked up. 'Better?'

'Much.' Amy nodded.

'You should eat.'

She stared at the food spread before him and shook her head. 'I'm not hungry,' she lied.

'You do not decline when a king invites you to dine at his table.'

'Oh, but you do when that king has just declined *you*,' Amy responded. 'My rule.' And the strangest thing was she even managed a small smile as she said it—another smile that caught Emir by surprise.

'I thought you would be…' He did not really know. Emir had expected more hurt, but instead there was an air of peace around her that he had never noticed before.

'I really am fine,' Amy said. She was aware

there was a new fracture he had delivered to her heart, but it was too painful for examination just yet, so instead she explored past hurts. 'In fact I remembered something when I was riding,' Amy explained. 'Something I'd forgotten. I've been struggling with my memory—I couldn't remember the weeks before the accident.' She shook her head. 'It doesn't matter.'

She went again to head to her room, but again he called her back. 'You need to eat.' He held up a plate of *lokum* and Amy frowned at the pastry, at the selection of food in front of him.

'I thought it was just fruit that we could eat?'

'It is the twins who can eat only fruit and drink only water. I thought it better for them if we all did it.'

She saw the tension in his jaw as he spoke of the twins. Sometimes he sounded like a father— sometimes this dark, brooding King was the man she had once known.

'They will be okay.' He said it as if he was trying to convince himself.

'I'm sure they'll be fine,' Amy said. Tonight he was worried about his children. Tonight neither of them really wanted to be alone. 'I'll get changed and then I'll have something to eat.'

Was there relief in his eyes when he nodded?

There was not much to choose from—it was either her nightdress and dressing gown or yet another pale blue robe. Amy settled for the latter, brushed her damp hair and tied it back, and then headed out to him.

He was tired of seeing her in that robe. He wanted to see her in other colours—wanted to see her draped in red or emerald, wanted to see her hair loose around her shoulders and those full lips rouged. Or rather, Emir conceded as he caught the fresh, feminine scent of her as she sat down, he wanted to see the shoulders he had glimpsed moments earlier, wanted only the colour of her skin and her naked on the bed beneath him. But her revelation had denied them that chance.

'I apologise.' He came right out and said it. 'To have it happen to you twice...'

'Honestly...' Amy ate sweet pastry between words—she really was hungry. Perhaps for the first time in a year she knew what starving was. She'd been numb for so long and now it felt as if all her senses were returning. 'I'm okay.' She wondered how she might best explain what she was only just discovering herself. 'Since the accident I've felt like a victim.' It was terribly hard to express it! 'I didn't like feeling that way. It didn't feel like me. I didn't like my anger towards him.'

'You had every reason to be angry.'

'No,' Amy said. 'As it turns out, I didn't.'

'I don't understand.'

'There were a few days before I fully came round when I could hear conversations. I couldn't speak because I was on a machine.'

Emir watched her fingers go instinctively to her throat.

'That was when I heard the doctors discussing the surgery I'd had.' She was uncomfortable explaining things to him, so she kept it very brief. 'The horse had trampled me. They took me to surgery and they had to remove my ovaries. They left a small piece of one so that I didn't go into…'

'Menopause.' He said it for her, smiled because she was embarrassed, 'I do know about these things.'

'I know.' She squirmed. 'It just feels strange, speaking about it with you. Anyway, I lay there unable to speak and heard my fiancé talking to his mother—how he didn't know what to do, how he'd always wanted children. Later, after I was discharged from the hospital, he told me it was over, that he'd been having doubts for ages, that it wasn't about the accident. But I knew it was. Or rather I thought I knew it was.' She looked up at Emir's frown. 'When I was riding today I remembered the last time I rode a horse. I don't remember falling off, or being trampled, but I do remember what I was thinking. I was unhappy, Emir.' She admitted it out loud for the first time, for even back then she had kept it in. 'I felt trapped and I was wondering how I could call off the wedding. That was what I was thinking when the accident happened—he was right to end things. It wasn't working. I just didn't know it—till now.'

'You didn't love him?' Emir asked, and watched as she shook her head. As she did so a curl escaped the confines of the hair tie. He was jealous of her fingers as they caught it and twisted it as she pondered his question.

'I did love him,' she said slowly, for she was still working things out for herself, still piecing her life together. 'But it wasn't the kind of love I wanted. We'd been going out together since we were teenagers. Our engagement seemed a natural progression—we both wanted children, we both wanted the same things, or thought we did. I cared for him and, yes, I suppose I loved him. But it wasn't…' She couldn't articulate the word. 'It wasn't a passionate love,' Amy attempted. 'It was…' She still couldn't place the word.

Emir tried for her. 'Safe?'

But that wasn't the word she was looking for either.

'Logical,' Amy said. 'It was a sort of logical love. Does that make sense?'

'I think so,' Emir said. 'That is the kind of love we build on here—two people who are chosen, who are considered a suitable match, and then love grows.'

He was quiet for a moment. The conversation was so personal she felt she could ask. 'Was that the love you had with Hannah?'

'Very much so,' Emir said. 'She was a wonderful wife, and would have been an amazing mother as well as a dignified sheikha queen.'

Amy heard the love in his voice when he spoke of her and they were not jealous tears that she blinked back. 'Maybe my fiancé and I would have made it.' Amy gave a tight shrug. 'I'm quite sure we would have had a good marriage. I think I was chasing the dream—a home and children, doing things differently than my parents.'

'A grown-up dolls' house?' Emir suggested, and she smiled.

'I guess I just wanted…' She still didn't know the word for it.

'An illogical love?' Emir offered—and that was it.

'I did,' Amy said, and then she stood. 'I do.'

'Stay,' he said. 'I have not explained.'

'You don't need to explain, Emir,' Amy said. 'I know we can't go anywhere. I know it is imperative to your country's survival that you have a son.' But there was just a tiny flare of hope. 'Could you speak to King Rakhal and have the rule revoked?' Amy didn't care if she was speaking out of turn. 'It is a different time now.'

'Rakhal's mother died in childbirth,' Emir said. 'And, as I told you, for a while her baby was not expected to survive. The King of Alzirz came to my father and asked the same…' Emir shrugged his broad shoulders. 'Of course my father declined his request. He wanted the countries to be one.'

'You've thought about it, then?'

He looked at her and for the first time revealed to another person just a little of what was on his mind. 'I have more than thought about it. I approached Rakhal when my wife first became ill. His response was as you might expect.' He shook his head as he recalled that conversation. Could see again the smirk on Rakhal's face when he had broached the subject. How he had relished Emir's rare discomfort. How he had enjoyed watching a proud king reduced to plead.

Emir looked into Amy's blue eyes and somehow the chill in him thawed slightly. He revealed more of the burden that weighed heavily on his mind. 'I have thought about many things, and I am trying to make the best decision not just for my country but for my daughters.' He had said too much. Immediately Emir knew that. For no one must know everything.

She persisted. 'If you didn't have a son...'

'It would be unthinkable,' Emir said. And yet it was all he thought about. He looked to her pale blue eyes and maybe it was the wind and the sound of the desert, perhaps the dance of the shadows on the walls, but he wanted to tell her—wanted to take her to the dark place in his mind, to share it. But he halted, for he could not. 'I *will* have a son.' Which meant his bride could not be her. 'Marriage means different things for me. I am sorry if I hurt you—that was never my intention.'

'I didn't take it personally...' But at the last moment her voice broke—because her last words weren't true. She'd realised it as she said them. It was a very personal hurt, and one to be explored only in private, in the safety of her room. There she could cry at this very new loss. 'Goodnight, Emir.'

'Amy?'

She wished he would not call her back, but this time it was not to dissuade her. Instead he warned her what the night would bring.

'The wind is fierce tonight—she knows that you are new here and will play tricks with your mind.'

'You talk about the wind as if it's a person.'

'Some say she is a collection of souls.' He saw her instantly dismiss that. 'Just don't be alarmed.'

She wasn't—at first.

Amy lay in the bed and stared at the ceiling—a ceiling that rose and fell with the wind. She missed the girls more than she had ever thought possible and she missed too what might have been.

Not once had she glimpsed what Emir had been considering—not once had she thought herself a potential sheikha queen. She'd thought she might be his mistress—an occasional lover, perhaps, and a proxy mother to the twins.

Emir had been willing to marry her.

It helped that he had.

It killed that he never could.

Amy lay there and fought not to cry—not that he would be able to hear her, for the wind was whipping around the tent and had the walls and roof lifting. The flickering candles made the shadows dance as if the room were moving, so she closed her eyes and willed sleep to come. But the wind shrieked louder, and it sounded at times like the twins. She wept for them.

Later she could hear a woman screaming—the same sound she had heard the night they were born. The shouts had filled the palace a year ago this night, when the twins were being born. These screams sounded like a woman birthing—screams she would never know—and it was torture. She knew the wind played tricks, but the screams and the cries were more than she could bear.

Maybe they'd taunted Emir too, for when she opened her eyes he was standing there, still robed, his sword strapped to his hips. His *kafeya* was off. He stood watching, a dark shadow in the night, but one that did not terrify.

'When you kissed me back, when you said *please*, what did you think I meant?' he asked.

'I thought it was sex that was on offer.' If she sounded coarse she didn't care. Her hurt was too raw to smother it with lies.

'That is not our way.' Emir looked at her. 'In Alzirz they are looser with their morals. There are harems and…' He shook his head. 'I did not want that for you.'

Not for the first time, but for more shame-

ful reasons now, she wished she were there—
wished it was there that Emir was King.

'I never for a moment thought you would consider me for your bride. When we kissed—when
we...' She swallowed, because it was brutal to
her senses to recall it. 'When we kissed,' Amy
started again, 'when we touched...' Her eyes
were brave enough to meet his. 'I wasn't thinking about the future or the twins or solutions, I
thought it was just me that you wanted...'

And he looked at her, and the winds were si-
lenced. The screams and the tears seemed to
halt. Surely for one night he could think like a
man and not a king? Emir was honest in his response and his voice was low with passion. 'It
was,' Emir said. Yes, at first he had been seduc-
ing, but later... 'When I kissed you I forgot.'

'Forgot?'

'I forgot everything but you.'

She looked over to him, saw the raw need in
his eyes, saw the coffee colour of his skin and

the arms that had held her, and she wanted his mouth back.

'I know we can't go anywhere. I know…' She just wanted to be a woman again—wanted one time with this astonishingly beautiful man. 'Just once…' she whispered, and Emir nodded.

'Just once,' came his reply, for that was all it must be, and with that he picked her up and carried her to his bed.

CHAPTER SEVEN

SHE lay on his bed and watched as he undid the leather belt and the sword fell to the floor with a gentle thud. She turned away from him then, for she was filled with terror. All too clearly she could see his braids and royal decorations and she knew what they were doing was wrong—she wanted the man, not the King, and his status was truly terrifying.

'Turn around,' Emir told her.

Slowly she did so, and saw him naked, and she feared that too—for he was more beautiful then she had even imagined and, yes, now it was safe to admit to herself that she had imagined. He hardened under her gaze. Her shy eyes took in more of him—the toned planes of his stomach, the long, solid thighs and the arms she now ached to have hold her again.

'This is wrong,' she said as he walked towards her.

'It doesn't feel wrong,' he said, and he climbed in beside her. The fact that the bodies that met were forbidden to each other only heightened their desire.

She cringed as he took off her nightgown, closed her eyes as he pushed down the bedclothes and fully exposed her. He wanted to know every piece of her skin. He kissed not her mouth but the breast that he had so nearly kissed in the desert, and she was as aroused in that instant as she had been then. She returned to that moment in the desert when he could have taken her. He kissed lower, kissed her stomach as deeply as if it were her mouth, and then he moved lower still, and she lay there writhing as he made her feel like a woman again.

Her body had craved passion for so long and

he had returned it to her. She had denied herself touch, had felt untouchable, empty, and now he filled her with his tongue, touched her so intimately and not with haste.

With her moans he grew.

With her screams he lost himself more.

He had shared not an ounce of emotion since the death of his wife, but he shared it now.

There was a burden for this King that not the wisest of his council knew about. There was a decision in the making that he could only come to alone—a decision he had wrestled with for more than a year now. It was all forgotten.

He felt her fingers in his hair and the tightening of her thighs to his head. Her hips attempted to rise but he pushed her down with his mouth till she throbbed into him, and then he could wait no more.

He kneeled, looked down at all that beckoned, and she felt the roughness of his thighs part her legs further. Her body still quivered from his intimate exploration as he parted her with his thumbs. She looked with decadent, wanton fear at what would soon be deep inside her and, breathless, pleaded for it to be *now*.

He pulled back, for he must sheathe, and then he heard her whisper.

'We don't have to.'

For the first time, the fact that there could be no baby brought only relief, for neither wanted to halt things.

Now he lifted her hips, aimed himself towards her. A more deliberate lover he could not be, for he watched and manoeuvred every detail, and she let him—let him position her till he was poised at her entrance, and then he made her wait.

'Emir…'

His smile was as rare as it was wicked.

'Emir…'

He hovered closer and was cruel in his timing; that beat of space made her weep, and her mouth opened to beg him again, but her words faded as he filled her, as he drove into her with the ardour of a man ending his deprivation. He forgot his size and to be gentle, and never had she been so grateful to have a man forget.

He filled her completely, and then filled her again. He was over her, and the kiss he had first denied her was Amy's reward, for he hushed her moans with his mouth until it was Emir who could not be silent. The pleasure was now his, all pain obliterated, the shackles temporarily released. His mind soared in freedom as her body moved with his. Escape beckoned and he claimed it, groaning to hold on to it, yearning to sustain it. But the pulse of her around him was too much—the rapid tightening and flicker of intimate muscles, her hot wet cheek next to his, her breath, his name in his ear.

He lost himself to her, gave in to what was and spilled into her, called out her name as they dived into pleasure. The wind was their friend now, for it shrieked louder around them, carried their shouts and their moans and buried their secret in the sands.

CHAPTER EIGHT

OF COURSE it should never have happened.

And of course it must never be referred to again.

But it was a little before morning and they'd made love again after she'd turned and looked at him while she still could. She ran a finger across the scar above his eye about which she had often wondered and was brave enough now to ask.

'What is that from?'

'You don't ask that sort of thing.'

'Naked beside you I do.'

Maybe it was better she knew, Emir thought. Maybe then she could understand how impossible it was for them.

'Some rebels decided that they could not wait for the predictions, so they took matters into their own hands.' He did not look at her as he spoke. He felt her fingers over his scar and re-membered again. 'They decided to take out one lineage.' He heard her shocked gasp. 'Of course our people had seen them approaching and they rallied. My father went out and battled, as did my brother and I…'

'And your mother?'

'She was killed in her bed.'

He removed her hand from his face, climbed out of bed, and dressed and headed to prayer. He had begged the desert for a solution and for a moment had thought one had been delivered; instead it had been a taunt. He must play by the rules, Emir realised as he remembered again that night and all he had inherited.

So he prayed for his country and his people.

He must forget about their lovemaking, the woman he had held in his arms. He had never felt closer to another, even Hannah, and he prayed for forgiveness.

He prayed for his daughters and the decision he was making and he got no comfort, for his heart still told him he was making the wrong one.

Then he remembered what his father had fought for and he knew he must honour it—so he prayed again for his country.

Amy lay silent, taking in this last time she would be in his bed, the masculine scent of him. Her hand moved to the warm area where he had slept and she yearned to wait for him to return to the bed and make love to her just one more time. But for both of them that would be unfair, so she headed to the bathing area and then to her own room.

She fixed her hair and put on the blue robe, became the nanny again.

For Emir there was both regret and relief when he returned from prayer and saw the empty bed. Regret and relief as they shared a quiet breakfast. She did not once refer to last night, but it killed him to see her in the familiar blue robe and to know what was beneath.

And when the silence deafened her, when she knew if she met his eyes just one more time, it would end in a kiss she wished him good morning and headed to her room. She lay on her bed and willed the twins to return, for sanity to come back to her life and to resume again her role.

But of course it felt different.

Her heart swelled with pride and relief when the birthday girls were returned.

Their squeals of delight as she kissed them made her eyes burn from the salt of unshed tears. She realised how close to being their mother she had come.

'What are these?' She attempted normal conversation, looked at the heart-shaped vials that now hung around their necks.

'They are filled with the sands of the desert— they must be worn till they go to bed tonight, then they are to be locked away until their wedding day.'

'They're gorgeous.' Amy held one between her finger and thumb. 'What are they for?'

'Fertility.' He almost spat the word out, his mood as dark as it had been the morning she had faced him in his office, and it didn't improve as they boarded the helicopter for their return to the palace.

The twins were crying as the helicopter took off.

'They are not to arrive with teary faces. There will be many people gathered to greet them. My people will line the streets.'

'Then comfort them!' Amy said, but his face was as hard as granite and he turned to the window. 'Emir, please.' Amy spoke when perhaps she should not, but he had been so much better with the girls yesterday, and it worried her that she had made things worse instead of better. 'Please don't let last night…'

He looked over to Amy, his eyes silencing her, warning her not to continue, and then he made things exceptionally clear. 'Do you really think what happened last night might have any bearing on the way I am with my daughters?' He mocked her with one small incredulous shake of his head. 'You are the nanny—you are in my country and you have to accept our laws and our ways. They are to be stoic. They are to be strong.'

But he did take Clemira and hold her on his knees, and when Clemira was quiet so too was Nakia.

Amy sat silent, craning her neck as the palace loomed into view, bouncing Nakia on her knee, ready to point out all the people, to tell the little girl that the waving flags were for her sister and herself.

Except the streets were empty.

She looked to Emir. His face was still set in stone and he said nothing.

He strode from the helicopter, which left Amy to struggle with the twins. He was greeted by Patel and whatever was said was clearly not good news, for Emir's already severe expression hardened even more.

Amy had no idea what was happening.

She took the twins to the nursery and waited for information, to find out what time the party would be, but with each passing hour any hope of celebration faded and again it was left to Amy to amuse the little girls on what should be the happiest of days.

Her heart was heavy in her chest and she fought back tears as she made them cupcakes in the small kitchen annexe. At supper time she sang 'Happy Birthday' to them, watched them smile in glee as they opened the presents she had wrapped for them. Amy smiled back—but her face froze when she saw Emir standing in the nursery doorway.

His eyes took in the presents, the teddies and the DVDs. He watched as Amy walked over to him, her face white with fury, and for a second he thought she might spit.

'They have everything, do they?' Her eyes challenged him. 'Some party!'

'My brother is too busy in Dubai with his horses.'

He walked over to the twins and kissed the two little dark heads. He spoke in his language to them for a few moments. 'I have their present.'

He called the servants to come in and Amy watched as the delighted twins pulled paper off a huge parcel. She bit on her lip when she saw it was a dolls' house—an exquisite one—built like the palace, with the stairs, the doors, the bedroom.

'I thought about what you said. How it helped you. I wanted the same for them.'

'How?' Even though it seemed like a lifetime ago, it had only been a couple of days. 'How on earth did you get this done so quickly?'

'There are some advantages to being King— though right now...' Emir almost smiled, almost met her eyes but did not '…I can't think of many.'

He stood from where he'd knelt with the twins and still could not look at her. He just cleared his throat and said what he had to—did what should have been done long ago.

'Fatima will be sharing in the care of the twins from now on,' Emir said, and Fatima stepped forward.

Not *assisting*, not *helping*, Amy noted.

'She speaks only a little English and she will speak none to the twins: they need to learn our ways now.'

She did not understand what had happened. For as blissful as last night had been she would give it back, would completely delete it, if it had changed things so badly for the girls.

'Emir…' She saw Fatima frown at the familiarity. 'I mean, Your Highness…'

But he didn't allow her to speak, to question, just walked from the nursery, not turning as the twins started to cry. Amy rushed to them.

'Leave them,' Fatima said.

'They're upset.' Amy stood her ground. 'It's been a long day for them.'

'It's been a long day for their country,' Fatima responded. 'It is not just the twins who will mark today—Queen Natasha gave birth to a son at sunrise.'

For a bizarre moment Amy thought of the screams she had heard last night, the cries she had thought might come from Hannah. Yet Natasha had been screaming too. She felt as if the winds were still tricking her, that the desert was always one step ahead, and watched as Fatima picked up the twins and took them to their cots. Fatima turned to go, happy to leave them to cry.

That was why there had been no celebrations, no crowds gathering in the streets. It had been a silent protest from the people—a reminder to their King that he must give them a son. Fatima confirmed it as she switched out the light.

'Unlike Alzan, the future of Alzirz is assured.'

CHAPTER NINE

'THEY won't stay quiet for that length of time unless you are holding them.'

It had been a long morning for Amy. They were practising the formalities for the new Prince's naming ceremony tomorrow, and as it was Fatima who would be travelling with the King and the Princesses, Amy had been tidying the nursery. The windows were open and she had heard their little protests, their cries to be held by their father and eventually, reluctantly, Emir had asked for Amy to be sent down.

'Fatima will be the one holding them.'

'They want you.'

'They cannot have me,' Emir said. She caught his eye then and he saw her lips tighten, because, yes, she knew how that felt. 'I will be in military uniform. I have to salute.' He stopped explaining then—not just because he'd remembered that he didn't have to, but because Nakia, who had been begging for his arms, now held her arms out to Amy. They both knew that there would be no problem if it was Amy who was travelling with him.

Not that Emir would admit it.

Not that she wanted to go.

She could not stand to be around him—could not bear to see the man she loved so cold and distant, not just with her but with the babies who craved his love.

'Can you hold *one*?' She tried to keep the exasperation from her voice as she hugged a tearful Clemira.

'I've tried that. Clemira was jealous,' he explained as Fatima sloped off with Nakia to get her a drink.

'If you can hold one then it needs to be Clemira. Keep Clemira happy and then usually Nakia is fine.' She saw him frown and she could not check her temper because he didn't know something so basic about his own daughters. 'Just hold Clemira,' she said, handing the little girl to him. 'God, it's like I'm speaking in a foreign language.'

'It is one to me!' Emir hissed, and she knew they were not talking about words.

Amy walked off, back to the palace, so she could listen to more tears from the window and do nothing, back to a role that was being eroded by the minute. She looked at the dolls' house and felt like kicking it, felt like ripping down the palace walls, but she stifled a laugh rather than turn into psycho-nanny. She polished the tables in the nursery and changed the sheets, tried to pretend she was working.

'It worked.'

She turned around at the sound of him, stood and stared. He held the twins, both asleep, their heads resting on his shoulders. She waited for Fatima to appear, except she didn't.

'Fatima is getting a headache tablet.' Emir gave a wry smile. 'I said I would bring them up.'

How sad that this was so rare, Amy reminded herself. How sad that something so normal merited an explanation—and, no, she told herself, she did *not* want him.

He went to put Clemira down and she moved to help him.

'I don't know how...' It was almost an apology.

'No.' She took one child from his arms. 'I can't put them down together now either,' she said. 'They're far too big for that.' She lowered Clemira to the mattress as Emir did the same with Nakia. 'It was easier when they were little.' She was jabbering now. 'But I've had to lower the mattress now they're standing.' She could feel him watching her mouth; she feared to look at him—just wanted Fatima to come.

'Amy...'

'They're enjoying the dolls' house.'

She kept her head down because she knew what would happen if she lifted it. She knew because it had almost happened the day before, and the day before that—moments when it had been impossible to deny, when it had almost killed not to touch, when it would have been easier to give in. But if she kissed him now this was what they would be reduced to—furtive snogs when Fatima wasn't around, a quick shag when no one was watching, perhaps? And she was better than that, Amy told herself.

But the tears were coming. She reminded herself that, even if she was crying she was strong.

It was Amy who walked out. Amy who left him watching his children as she headed to her room,

'You need to come home.'

Rather than cry she rang home, desperate for normality, for advice. Though Amy's mum didn't know all that had gone on, even if she did, Amy realised, her advice would be the same.

'Amy, you're not going to change things there. I told you that when you accepted the job.'

'But Queen Hannah…'

'Is dead.'

The harsh words hit home.

'Even Queen Hannah knew that the country would have little time for her daughters. That was why she wanted them to be educated in England.'

'I can't leave them.'

'You have no choice,' her mum said. 'Can you really stand another three years of this?'

No, Amy could not. She knew that as she hung up the phone. The last ten days had been hell. With the anniversary of Queen Hannah's death approaching the palace was subdued, but more than that, worse was to come, for there would be a wedding in a few weeks and how could she be here for that?

She couldn't.

Rather than being upset, Amy had actually been relieved that Fatima had been selected to travel with the King. She had decided that the time she would spend alone must be used wisely, but really her decision was made.

Her mother was right: she had no choice but to go home.

She had to, she told herself as she made it through another night.

By morning, she was already wavering.

She walked into the nursery where two beaming girls stood in their cots and blew kisses. They wriggled and blew bubbles as she bathed them, spat out their food and hated their new dresses, pulled out the little hair ribbons faster than Fatima could tie them.

Amy knew every new tooth in their heads, every smile was a gift for her, and she could not stand to walk away.

Except she had to.

Amy packed cases for the little girls, putting in their swimming costumes, because she knew there were several pools at the Alzirz palace.

'They won't be needing those,' Fatima said. 'I shall not be swimming with them.'

And their father certainly wouldn't, Amy thought, biting down on her lip as she struggled to maintain her composure.

She helped Fatima bring them down to wait for the King and board the helicopter.

'Be good!' Amy smiled at the girls when she wanted to kiss them and hold them. She was terribly aware that this might be the last time she would see them, that perhaps it would be kinder to all of them for her simply to leave while they were away.

As Emir strode across the palace he barely glanced at his daughters, and certainly he did not look in Amy's direction. He was dressed in military uniform as this was to be a formal event and she loathed the fact that this man still moved her. His long leather boots rang out as he walked briskly across the marble floor, only halting when Patel called out to him.

'La.' He shook his head, his reply instant, and carried on walking, but Patel called to him again and there was a brief, rather urgent discussion. Then Emir headed into his study, with Patel following closely behind.

'I'll say goodbye now!' Amy spoke to the girls, for they were getting increasingly fretful and so too was she. She must remember that they were not her babies, that they would be fine with Fatima, that they were not hers to love. But it killed her to turn around and walk up the grand staircase. It was almost impossible not to look around and respond to their tears, but she did her level best—freezing on the spot when she heard Patel's voice.

'The King wishes to speak with you.'

'Me?' Slowly Amy turned around.

'Now,' Patel informed her. 'He is busy—do not keep him waiting.'

It felt like the longest walk of her life. Amy could feel eyes on her as she walked back down the stairs, trying to quieten her mind, trying not to pre-empt what Emir wanted though her heart surely knew. She had never been summoned to speak to him before, and could only conclude that his thoughts were the same as hers—while he was gone, perhaps it was better that she leave.

It was terribly awkward to face him. Not since their night together had it been just them, for Fatima was always around, her silent criticism following Amy's every move. There was no discomfort in Emir, she noted. He looked as uninterested and as imposing as he had the last time that she had stood there, and his voice was flat.

'*You* are to accompany the children to the naming ceremony of the new Prince of Alzirz.'

'Me?' Amy swallowed. This was so not what she had been expecting. 'But I thought it was considered more suitable for Fatima to travel with them? She is more well-versed—'

'This is not a discussion,' Emir interrupted. 'You are to go now and to pack quickly. The helicopter is waiting and I have no intention of arriving late.'

'But—' She didn't understand the change of plan. She needed this time alone and was nervous about travelling with him.

'That will be all,' Emir broke in. 'As I said, I did not call you in here for a discussion.'

It was Patel who offered a brief explanation as she left the office. 'Queen Natasha wishes to discuss English nannies and has said she is looking forward to speaking with you.'

This made sense, because of course a request from Queen Natasha during the new Prince's naming ceremony must be accommodated.

It mattered not that it would break her heart.

Amy packed quickly. She selected three pale blue robes and her nightwear, and threw a few toiletries into her bag. Even if there was the heli-copter, the King and his entourage waiting, still she took a moment to pack the twins' swimming costumes and her own bikini—because, unlike Fatima, she *would* swim with the girls.

Emir was at the helicopter, and she felt his air of impatience as she stepped in. He had already strapped in the girls and Fatima gave Amy a long, cool look as she left the aircraft, for it was an honour indeed to travel with the King.

It was not the easiest of journeys, though Emir did hold Nakia as they neared their destina-tion. Again Amy watched his features harden and, looking out of the window, thought per-haps she understood why. Alzirz was celebrat-ing as Alzan should have been on the day of the twins' birthday. The streets around the palace were lined with excited people waving flags. They all watched in excitement as dignitaries arrived for the naming of their new Prince.

How it must kill him to be so polite, Amy

mused as they arrived at the palace and the two men kissed on both cheeks. She could feel the simmering hatred between them that went back generations.

Queen Natasha didn't seem to notice it. She was incredibly informal and greeted both Amy and the twins as if they were visiting relatives, rather than a nanny and two young princesses. 'They've grown!' she said.

She looked amazing, Amy noted, wearing a loose fitting white robe embroidered with flowers. She certainly didn't look like a woman who had given birth just a few days ago, and Amy felt drab beside her.

'Come through!' Natasha offered, seeing the twins were more than a little overawed by the large formal gathering. 'I'll take you to the nursery. I have to get the baby ready.' She chatted easily as they walked through the palace. 'I'll introduce you to my nanny, Kuma. She's just delightful, but I really want him to learn English.'

She smiled over to Amy. 'You're not looking for a job, by any chance?' she asked shamelessly.

'I'm very happy where I am,' came Amy's appropriate response, though she was tempted to joke that Natasha might find her on the palace doorstep in a couple of days. But, no, Amy realised, even if Natasha *was* nice, even if she *was* easy to talk to, in Alzirz as in Alzan the Royal Nanny would have to be obedient to royal command. She could never put her heart through this again.

Kuma really was delightful. She was far more effusive and loving than Fatima. She smiled widely when she saw the twins, put a finger up to her lips to tell them to hush, and then beckoned them over to admire the new prince. Nakia wasn't particularly interested, but Clemira clapped her hands in delight and nearly jumped out of Amy's arms in an effort to get to the baby. She was clearly totally infatuated with the young Prince.

'He's beautiful,' Amy said. His skin was as dark as Rakhal's, but his hair was blonde like Natasha's, and Amy was suddenly filled with hopeless wonder as to what *her* babies might have been like if Emir was their father. She was consumed again with all she had lost, but then she held Clemira tighter and qualified that—all that she was losing by walking away.

'Would you like to hold him?' Natasha offered.

'He's asleep,' Amy said, because she was terrified if she did that she might break down.

'He has to get up, I'm afraid,' Natasha said. 'I want to feed him before the naming ceremony.' She scooped the sleeping infant out of his crib and, as Kuma took Clemira, handed him to Amy.

Sometimes it had hurt to hold Clemira and Nakia in those early days, to know that she would never hold her own newborn, and the pain was back now, as acute as it had been then, perhaps more so—especially when the two Kings came in. Rakhal was proud and smiling down at his son. Emir was polite as he admired the new Prince. But there was grief in his eyes and Amy could see it. She was angry on behalf of his girls, yet she understood it too—for the laws in this land, like in the desert, could be cruel.

'Come,' Emir told her, 'we should take our places.'

Her place was beside him—for the last time.

She stood where in the future she would not: holding his daughters. She held Clemira and sometimes swapped. Sometimes he held both, when he did not have to salute, so he could give Amy a rest and once, when they girls got restless, she set them on the ground, for it was a long and complicated ceremony.

'They did well,' Emir said as they walked back to the nursery with the weary twins.

'Of course they did!' Amy smiled. 'And if they'd cried would it really have mattered? Tariq screamed the whole ceremony.'

'He did.' Emir had been thinking the same,

knew he must not be so rigid. Except his country expected so little from his daughters and somehow he wanted to show them all they could be. 'Just so you know, the Alzirz nanny will be looking after the twins tonight. They are to make a brief appearance at the party, but she will dress them and take care of that.'

'Why?' Amy asked, and she watched his lips tighten as she questioned him.

'Because.' Emir answered, and he almost hissed in irritation as he felt her blue eyes still questioning him. He refused to admit that he did not know why.

'Because what?'

He wanted to turn around and tell her that he was new to this, that the intricacies of parenthood and royal protocol confused him at times too. Hannah would have been the one handling such things. It was on days like today that the duty of being a single parent was the hardest. Yet he could not say all this, so his voice was brusque when he conceded to respond. 'Sheikha Queen Natasha wants them to be close. It is how things are done. If Prince Tariq comes to stay in Alzan you will look after him for the night.'

'I thought you were rivals?'

'Of course,' Emir said. 'But Queen Natasha is new to this. She does not understand how deep the rivalry is, that though we speak and laugh and attend each other's celebrations there is no affection there.'

'None?'

'None.' His face was dark. 'The twins will be looked after by their nanny tonight. They will be brought back to you in the morning and you will all join me at the formal breakfast tomorrow.'

'But the girls will be unsettled in a new...'

He looked at her. He must have been mad to even have considered it—crazy even to think it. For she would not make a good sheikha queen. There was not one sentence he uttered that went unquestioned, not a thought in her head that she did not voice.

'You keep requesting a night off. Why then, do you complain when you get one?'

Amy reminded herself of her place.

'I'm not complaining.' She gave him a wide smile. 'I'm delighted to have a night off work. I just wasn't expecting it.'

'You can ring down for dinner to be sent to you.'

'Room service?' Amy kept that smile, remembered her place. 'And I've got my own pool... Enjoy the party.'

Of course he did not.

He was less than happy as he took his place at the gathering. He could see the changes Natasha had brought to the rather staid palace, heard laughter in the air and the hum of pleasant, relaxed conversation, and it only served to make him more tense. He held his daughters along with Kuma, and Natasha held her son. He saw

Kuma being so good with them and thought perhaps Fatima was not so suitable.

Maybe a gentler nanny would suit the children best, Emir thought. For he knew that Amy was leaving—had seen it in her eyes—and he held Clemira just a touch tighter before he handed her back to Kuma. His heart twisted again, for they should not be in this world without their mother, and a king should not be worrying about hiring a new nanny.

There was the one big decision that weighed heavily, but there were others that must be made too: their nanny, their schooling, their language, their tears, their grief, their future. He must fathom it all unshared with another who loved them. As a single father he did not know how to be.

Black was his mind as the babies were taken upstairs to the nursery, and he looked over to Rakhal, who stood with his wife by his side. Never had he felt more alone. Tonight he grieved the loss of both Hannah and Amy, and he was so distracted that he did not notice Natasha had made her way over.

'I'm sorry. This must be so difficult for you.'

He shot her a look of scorn. How dared she suggest to his face such a thing? How dared she so blatantly disrespect his girls?

But just as his mouth formed a scathing retort she continued. 'It's Hannah's anniversary soon?'

He closed his eyes for a second. Grief consumed him.

He nodded. 'She is missed.'

Natasha looked at this King with grief in his eyes, who stood apart and polite but alone. 'Where's Amy?'

'She is enjoying a night off,' he clipped, for he did not like to think about her when he wanted her here at his side.

'I didn't mean for her to stay in her room.' Natasha laughed. 'When I said that my nanny would look after the girls I was hoping that she would join us.'

'She is the nanny,' Emir said curtly. 'She is here only to look after the children.'

'Ah, but she's English,' Natasha sighed and rolled her eyes. 'Have you any idea how nice it feels to have someone here who is from home? I was so looking forward to speaking with her— we never really got a chance earlier.'

'She will bring the twins to breakfast tomorrow,' Emir responded, uncomfortable with such overt friendliness.

When he visited Alzirz, or when duty dictated that Rakhal visit Alzan, there were firm boundaries in place, certain ways things were done, but Natasha seemed completely oblivious to them. The new Sheikha Queen did not seem to understand that it was all an act between himself and Rakhal, that there was still a deep rivalry between the two Kings, born from an innate need to protect the kingdoms, their land and their people. Natasha simply didn't understand that although they spoke politely, although they attended all necessary functions, it was only mutual hate that truly united them.

'I'll have somebody sent to get her,' Natasha persisted.

Emir could only imagine how well that would go down with Amy. She didn't like to be told what to do at the best of times, and this certainly wasn't the best of times.

'She is staff,' Emir said, and that should have ended the conversation—especially as Rakhal had now come over. At least Rakhal knew how things were done. He would terminate this conversation in an instant, would quickly realise that lines were being crossed—unlike this beaming Englishwoman.

What *was* it with them?

Natasha smiled up to her husband. 'I was just saying to Emir that I was hoping to have Amy join us tonight. I do miss having someone from home to chat to at times.'

And love must have softened Rakhal's brain, Emir thought darkly, for instead of looking to Emir, instead of gauging his response, instead of playing by the unspoken rules he looked to his wife.

'Then why don't you have someone go to the suite and see if she would care to join us?' he said. Only then did he address Emir. 'Normally Natasha's brother and his fiancée would be here tonight, to join in the celebrations, but they are in the UK for another family commitment and couldn't make it.'

Emir did not care. Emir had no desire to know why Natasha's brother and his fiancée could not be here. Had Rakhal forgotten for a moment that this was all a charade? That there was more hate in the air than the palatial ballroom could readily hold? For when he thought of his daughters, thought of his late wife and the rule Alzirz refused to revoke, Emir could happily pull his knife.

'It would be unfair to her.' Emir did his best to keep his voice even. 'She will have only her working clothes with her.'

'I'm not that mean.' Natasha smiled. 'I wouldn't do that to her. I'll have some clothes and maidens sent to her room to help prepare her. I'll arrange it now.'

There was so much he would like to say—Emir was not used to having any decision questioned—and yet protocol dictated politeness even in this most uncomfortable of situations. He could just imagine Amy, in her present mood, if one of the servants were to knock at her door and insist that she come down and join in with the feasting and celebrations. A smile he was not expecting almost spread his lips at the very thought, but he rescued his features from expression and nodded to the waiting Queen.

'Very well, if you wish to have Amy here, I

shall go now and speak to her. I will ask her to come down, though she may already have retired for the night.'

Natasha smiled back at him and Emir could not understand why she could not see the hate in his eyes as he spoke. He strode out of the grand ballroom.

As he did so Rakhal turned to his wife. 'You are meddling.'

'Of course I'm not,' Natasha lied.

But her husband knew her too well. He had had the teachings too and his wife seduced with her beauty, dazzled like the sun low in the desert. He knew his wife was plotting now.

'Natasha? You do *not* interfere in such things.'

'I'm not,' Natasha insisted. 'You have to work the room and I would like someone to talk to in my own language. Amy seems nice.'

But of course she *was* meddling. Natasha had seen King Emir's eyes linger a little too long on Amy at times, when the nanny hadn't been aware he was watching her. She had seen the sadness behind his eyes too. And, yes, perhaps it was for selfish reasons also that she was interfering just a little, but the thought of someone from her own land to be beside her at these endless functions…

She knew that Emir must soon take a new sheikha queen, and if that queen happened to be Amy—well, who could blame her for giving Cupid a little nudge? She loved her new country—loved it so much—but the rivalry between the two nations, the bitterness between them and all the impossible rules she simply could not abide, and she was quite sure that Amy must feel the same.

Amy had not retired for the night as Emir was silently hoping as he walked through the palace to her room.

She had rung down for dinner and enjoyed a delicious feast—or tried to. She had been thinking about the girls, thinking about Emir and trying to picture her future without them. But it was too hard. So she had telephoned home, hoping for a long chat, but everybody must be at work because she had spoken to endless answering machines. And, yes, a night off was what she had asked for, and the Alzirz palace was as sumptuous as even the most luxurious hotel, but after an hour or two of reading and painting her toenails she had grown restless. Simply because it was there for the taking Amy put on her bikini and went for a long swim in her own private pool.

It was glorious—the temperature of the water perfect, the area shaded with date palms for complete privacy and protection from the fierce Alzirz sun during the day. Lying on her back, she could see the stars peeking through. But just as she started to relax, just as she had convinced herself to stop worrying about leaving Alzan, at least for tonight, she heard a bell ring from her suite.

Perhaps the maid had come to take her tray, Amy thought and, climbing out of the pool, went to answer the door. She had left her towel behind so she tied on a flimsy silk robe and called for the maid to come in. As the bell rang again Amy realised that perhaps she didn't understand English and opened the door—completely taken aback to find Emir standing there.

'It was not my intention to disturb you.' It was close to an apology, but not quite. He was a king summoning a servant, Emir reminded himself—it was a compliment in itself that he had come to her door. 'You are required downstairs.'

Amy frowned. 'Is there a problem with one of the twins?'

'Not at all.' He felt more than a little uncomfortable, especially as two damp triangles were becoming visible where her wet bikini seeped into the silk of her gown. 'Sheikha Queen Natasha has requested that you join in the celebrations.'

'No, thanks.' Amy gave a tight smile and went to close the door, but his booted foot halted it. 'Excuse me!' was Amy's brittle response.

'You don't understand,' Emir said, but he did remove his boot. 'That is why I came personally—to explain things to you. The Queen is hosting the party. It is the Queen who has requested you to come down, not me. It would be rude…'

'Rude for who?' Amy responded—because she did not want to go down there, did not want to be Natasha's little project for the night. She particularly did not want to spend any more time with Emir than she had to—things were already difficult enough.

Now he was at her door, and she could feel the cool wetness of her gown, knew from the flick of his eyes downwards that he had seen it too—that she might just as well not be wearing it. She was frantic to have him gone.

'It's rude to give me a night off and then revoke it!' She went to close the door again, did not want to prolong this discussion.

Emir would not let things be, and unless she slammed the door in his face she'd have to stand there and listen as he spoke on.

'If the twins were awake you would be expected to bring them down.'

'The twins are not in my care tonight.'

'That is not the point.' Emir's voice was stern. He was less than impressed with Amy's behaviour—especially as a maid came into the corridor and bowed her head to him. He stood there bristling with indignation as she went in and retrieved Amy's dinner tray. 'It is not right for me to be seen standing here and arguing with...'

'An employee?' she finished for him. But she accepted it was not fitting behaviour, and once the maid had gone she held the door further open for him. 'I have nothing to wear to a party. I haven't showered. I'm not ready...'

'That is being taken care of.' He blocked her

excuses as Natasha had blocked his. 'Queen Natasha is having some clothes and some maidens sent here to your room.' He turned to go. 'I expect you to be down there within half an hour.'

'Emir…'

There was a plea in her voice, a plea he had heard once before—the sound of her begging. He remembered her writhing beneath him and he hardly dared turn around.

'Don't make me do this. Go and enjoy the party on your own—make an excuse for me that is fitting. I don't know anything about…'

'Enjoy it?' He did turn around then, and he wished she were dressed—wished she looked anything other than she did now. For the gown was completely see-through. Three triangles taunted him. He could see the hard peaks of her nipples, see the flush on her neck. He should not be in this room with her for a whole set of reasons other than protocol. 'You will get dressed.'

When still she shook her head, he lost his temper. He spoke harsh angry words. It was far safer than pushing her onto the bed.

'You really think that I want to be down there? You really think that I'm enjoying making small talk, pretending that I do not hate them? If it were not for them…'

His black eyes met hers, as angry and savage as they had been the day she had first challenged him, but it did not scare her as it had then. His anger was not aimed at her, nor his words, Amy was quite sure. This would not be of his choosing, for this remote, private man to pour some of the pain out.

'Amy, please…'

Not once had he pleaded, not once that she knew of, and this came with a roar from the heart.

'I am asking you to please make this night easier for me—I am in hell down there.'

And he was. He was in hell tonight and no one knew. He could not share his burden; he carried it alone for he was King. He remembered his status and was ashamed of his words, his loss of control. But there was no smart retort from Amy. This time she stood stunned, as he was at his revelation, and he could see tears pooling in her eyes. She had glimpsed a little of his pain.

It was not that her mouth found his, nor was it his mouth which sought hers. Neither initiated the kiss. They simply joined, and he felt the bliss of oblivion. The pain ended for a moment and relief was instant. There was release and escape as her wet body pressed to his. He had craved her since that night, had wanted her each minute, and her tongue as it twisted with his, the heat of her skin through the damp gown, told him she had craved him as much.

She had.

His uniform was rough beneath her fingers, his mouth desperate on hers, his erection as fierce as his passion. She could feel him hard in her centre. It was happening again and it must not.

'Emir,' she whimpered, pulling her mouth back from his, though she did not want him to stop kissing her. Her lips ached for more as they moved from his. Regretting their departure, they returned, speaking into his mouth. 'We said just once.'

'Then get dressed,' he said, and his hands peeled off the damp robe, and his fingers worked the knot at the back of her bikini.

She moaned in his mouth as he stroked the aching peaks; his hands moved to her bottom and he pulled her up till her legs twined around him. This was way more than a kiss getting out of hand. The bed seemed an impossible distance, clothes their only barrier.

She felt the cold of brass buttons on her skin as he kissed her onto the bed, pulling at the damp bikini while his other hand moved to unbuckle his belt. And Amy realised her hands were helping his, for she was through with thinking. She could make decisions later, could work things out then. Right now she simply had to have him.

And she would have.

He would have had her.

Had the bell not rung again.

He looked down at where she lay, a breath away from coming. Regret was in both their eyes—not just at the interruption, but at what had taken place.

'That didn't just happen,' Amy said. Except it had. And now, even more so than before, it was impossible for her to stay.

No longer could their night in the desert be put down to a one-off. The attraction between them was undeniable and yet soon he would be taking a wife.

'It won't happen again,' Emir said.

They both knew he was lying.

He buckled up his belt, took her by the hand and led her to the bathroom. He checked his appearance in the mirror and then called to open the door. He watched as maidens bought in an array of clothing. He told them that Amy was in the shower and they must quickly prepare her to be brought down, and then he called out to her where she sat, crouched and shivering on the bathroom floor.

'You will get ready quickly.' He spoke as a king would when addressing a belligerent servant. He tried to remember his place and so too must she. 'Queen Natasha is waiting for you.'

CHAPTER TEN

'TOMORROW we leave for the desert.'

Natasha was irritating. She insisted on chatting as if they were old friends. And yet, Emir conceded, he would find *any* conversation annoying now, for his mind was only on Amy and what had just taken place.

Fool, he said to himself. Fool for not resisting. Fool for being weak.

And fool because tonight he would take her, only to lose her again in the morning.

Only to have her leave.

'I'm looking forward to it.' Natasha persisted with their one-way conversation. 'After all the celebrations and pomp surrounding the birth, it will be nice to get some peace.'

Now Emir did respond—and very deliberately

he chose to get things wrong. 'I'm sure that the Bedouins will take good care of him.' He saw the flare of horror in Natasha's eyes.

'Oh, it's not for that. It's way too soon to even *think* of being parted from him. That doesn't have to happen until he turns one.'

'*Before* he turns one,' Emir said, enjoying one pleasure in this night.

Two pleasures, he corrected, his mind drifting to Amy again. But he must stay focussed. He must concentrate on the conversation rather than anticipating her arrival, rather then remembering what had just happened. And perhaps it was time to give Natasha a taste of the medicine he had so recently sampled.

'I handed over the girls last week. Your husband was kind enough to grant a concession that they only stay in the desert for one night, given what happened to their mother.' He watched Natasha's lips tighten as he reminded her, none too gently, that her son would be in the desert for several nights—unless, of course, he lost his mother too. Unless he was forced to be weaned early, as Emir's daughters had been.

'How did the girls get on?' Natasha attempted to make it sound like a polite enquiry, as if she were asking after the girls rather than about what she could expect for her own son.

Emir knew that—it was the reason he didn't mollify her with his response. 'They screamed, they wept and they begged,' Emir said, watching as her face grew paler with each passing word. 'But they are the rules.' Emir shrugged. 'My daughters have been forced to be strong by circumstance, and so they survived it.'

He stopped twisting the knife then—not to save her from further distress, but because at that moment it seemed to Emir that everything simply stopped.

He had wondered far too often what Amy might look like out of that robe—he had pictured her not just in her nightdress, or naked beneath him, but dressed as his Queen.

She stepped into that vision now and claimed it, and deep in his gut a knife twisted.

She was dressed in a dark emerald velvet gown, her lips painted red and her eyes skilfully lined with kohl. Her hair was down. But nothing, not even the work of a skilled make-up artist, could temper the glitter in her eyes and the blush of her cheeks that their kiss had evoked. A riot of ringlets framed her face.

The world was cruel, Emir decided, for it taunted him with what he could not have. It showed him exactly how good it could have been, had the rules allowed her to join him, to be at his side.

Little more than a year ago she would have been veiled and hidden. A year ago he would not have had to suffer the tease of her beauty. But there was a new Sheikha Queen in Alizirz and times were changing.

Amy was changing.

Before his eyes, as she chatted with Natasha, he witnessed the effortless seduction of her body. For even as she turned slightly away from him her gestures seemed designed for him. She threw her head back and laughed, and then, as he knew it would, her hand instinctively moved to cover the scar on her throat. She twisted her hair around her fingers and he fought his desire to snake a hand around her waist. He wanted to join in the conversation as he would with a partner, to squeeze her waist just once to remind her that soon it would be over and soon they would be alone.

He put down the glass he was gripping rather than break it.

He turned away, but her laughter filled his ears.

Emir tried to remember the shy woman who had first entered the palace. He had not noticed her—or at least not in that way. His mind had been too consumed with worry for his wife, who had been fading by the day, for him to notice Amy. He wanted that back. He wanted the invisible woman she had been then.

But she wasn't invisible now.

She was there before his eyes.

And for her he might not be King.

'Thank you so much for coming down.' Natasha kissed Amy's cheek an agonising couple of hours later. 'It was lovely to talk.'

'It was my pleasure,' Amy said. 'Thank you for the invitation.'

She meant not a word.

And neither did Emir as he too politely thanked Rakhal and headed to the stairs.

She could not do this.

She stepped out into a fragrant garden, breathed in the blossom and begged it to quell the hammering of her mind. She listened to the fountain that should soothe. Except it did not, for she understood now a little of what Emir had meant about being in hell.

To stand apart while their minds were together, to ignore the other while their bodies silently screamed, was a potent taste of what might be to come when he married.

If she stayed.

Her fury was silent as she walked to her room, but she knew what she had to do. Her eyes took in the empty bed, but the scent of him confirmed that he was there. She saw that the doors were open and looked beyond them to where he stood by the pool. His jacket was undone and his eyes met hers. She shook her head, for forbidden lovers they must not be.

'No.'

Brave in her decision, she walked towards him, her anger building as she did so, reminding herself of all she did not admire about this man. She tried to dull the passion he triggered, determined that it be over.

'I'm through with this, Emir.' She made herself say it. 'I don't even like you.'

He simply looked.

His silence let her speak.

'I could never be with a man willing to ignore his children—despite my health problems, despite the fact I can't have children. Even without that I'd never have said yes.' She was lying, she could hear it, but her mind begged for it to be true. 'How can I love a man who doesn't care about his children?'

She watched his eyes narrow. Perhaps this was not the conversation he'd been expecting. It was a mistress he wanted, Amy reminded herself, not an argument about his children. But her racing heart surely stopped for a moment when his low voice delivered a response *she* was not expecting.

'Never say that.'

She thought he might throw the drink he was holding in her face. He might just as well have, because nothing could have shocked her more than the passion in his voice when his next words were delivered.

'I love my children.'

Except his actions did not show it, even if his words sounded true.

'You say that…'

'Trust that I have my daughters' best interests at heart.'

And she looked at his pain ravaged face and into eyes that glittered with the flames of hell. Somehow she did trust him. Despite all evidence to the contrary, she did believe him.

What did this man do to her? she begged of herself.

'Please, Emir, go.'

She could not think when he was around; she lost herself when he was near.

'Go,' she said, and walked to the bedroom.

'Go.' She sobbed as still by the pool he stood.

And she knew it was hopeless. For to leave he

would have to walk past her, and not to touch would be an impossible ask.

'Go.' She begged, even as she undressed for him, crying with shame at her own need.

She pulled down the zipper, slipped off the gown as he walked now towards her, her actions opposing her words as she removed her bra. Emir unbuckled his belt while entering the bedroom. Even then she shook her head. Even then she denied it as she took down her panties.

'No...' She changed her plea. She was sobbing as he kissed her down onto the bed, but she was grateful for the mattress that met her back for she got the gift of his full weight pressed into her. 'We mustn't...' She pushed at his bare chest but her fingers attempted to grip his skin, her nails wanted to dig in and leave her mark. 'Emir, you know that we mustn't...'

He took her hands and captured her wrists, held them over her head and hungrily kissed her.

Then with words he fought for what they both needed tonight. 'We must.'

His words were truthful, and he was fierce. Even naked he ruled her as he told her that he would make it work.

'We *will* be together…'

'There is no way…'

'I will find a way,' he told her. 'I will make this work. I will come to you in the night-time and in later years I will visit you and the girls in London.'

'Your mistress…?'

'More than a mistress,' he said between frantic kisses. 'You will care for the twins. You will raise them.'

Was it possible to love and hate at the same time?

To be filled with both want and loathing as he bound her to him, but with a life of lies?

He offered her everything, yet gave her nothing.

A life with no voice, Amy realised, and it was then that she found hers.

'No.'

His hands released their grip but she did not push him off. Instead she wrapped her arms around his back. 'This ends tonight.'

Their bodies knew that she lied.

All night he had been wanting her, and all night she had been waiting for him. They met now and their kisses tasted of fury for the future they could not have. She felt his anger as he stabbed inside her—anger at the rules that denied him the woman he wanted by his side. But for now there was an outlet, and he was animal. He bucked inside her and she lifted her hips to him. Their eyes locked in a strange loathing of what they might make the other do so easily. So easily she came to him.

And so deeply he delivered.

He knew she would shout. He felt her lungs fill and the tension in her throat as he shot into her; he felt her scream even as it rose, for his body and his soul knew her.

She came in a way she never had before, tightened in possession as he drove her further. She was grateful for his hand that smothered her mouth, furious that the only restraint he could muster was to stifle her screams with the hand she could never take.

She told herself she hated him.

Reminded herself she did not want to be his wife.

She was relieved it was over, surely?

They lay for a suitable while, waiting for normality to return, for the madness to subside, for him to rise from her bed and head to his own. But as he went to do so Amy's hand reached out to him and it was then that she cried, for she had proved that she lied.

Her fierce vow that it would end tonight had already been downgraded to the morning.

CHAPTER ELEVEN

MORNING came whether she wanted it to or not.

The sun did not care that it ended them.

It did what it was born to—it rose and dictated that their time was over.

She knew Emir was awake next to her. She watched the fingers of light spread across the floor and before they reached the bed she felt his hand on her hip, then her waist. She closed her eyes as he tucked her body towards him, felt his erection and wanted to wake every morning to him. She did not want to be a woman who settled for a slice of his life—didn't want to fit into allocated times. Yet had the phone not rung Amy knew that she would have.

'The twins are on their way.' Her voice was

urgent as she hung up, 'Kuma is bringing them now.'

There was no time for Emir to dress and leave, but he dealt with it instantly. Picking up the uniform he had so readily discarded last night, he headed to her en suite bathroom. This time it was he who hid there.

More than a little breathless, Amy searched for something to put on. Her panic was broken by a smile as a well-manicured hand appeared from the bathroom, holding her robe.

'You need to relax,' he warned her.

It was far easier said than done, because even as she tied the knot on her robe there was a knock on the door. When she opened it, there stood Kuma holding the smiling twins, who were clearly delighted to see Amy.

'They had a wonderful night,' Kuma explained, putting them down. The twins crawled happily in. 'Clemira is really taken with the new Prince, but I think they both want someone more familiar this morning. How was your night?' Kuma beamed. 'I hear you were asked to join in the celebrations.'

'I was.' Amy nodded, nervous and trying not to show it, attempting to carry on the conversation as if she *didn't* have the King of Alzan hiding in her room.

But thankfully Kuma did not prolong things. She wanted to get back to her young charge, so she wished Amy good morning and reminded her that the twins were expected to join the royals for breakfast in hour. 'I hope that your time in Alzirz has been pleasant,' Kuma said and then she was gone.

As was their time.

Like two homing devices, or observant kittens, the twins had made a beeline for the bathroom door, their dear little hands banging, calling out to the rather big secret behind it.

'She's gone.' Amy's face was burning as the door opened and out stepped Emir. She had expected him to be wearing his uniform, but instead he was dressed in a more standard thick white towelling robe.

'I will say that I'm looking for the twins if someone sees me in the corridor.' He had already worked out how to discard all evidence. 'If you can pack my uniform…?'

'Of course.' Amy nodded, telling herself that this was what it would be like were they to continue.

The twins let out a squeal of delight as they realised the two people they loved most in the world were together in the same room. And the man who had asked her to believe that he had his daughters' best interests at heart, even if he did not always show it, the man who so often did not reveal his feelings, confused her again as he picked up the girls and greeted them tenderly.

He went to hand them to Amy, but changed his mind.

'I hear you take them swimming at the palace?'

'Every day,' Amy said. 'They love it.'

Go, her eyes begged him.

'Show me,' he said.

And so she dressed them in their little costumes, put on yesterday's red bikini, and now he wasn't a distant sheikh king who watched from the poolside. Instead he made do with his surprisingly modern black hipsters and took to the water with his daughters.

Amy was suddenly shy.

It felt wrong at first to be in the water with him—wrong to join them, wrong when he splashed her, when he caught her unguarded, when he pulled her into the trio. But after a moment she joined in.

Amy knew what was wrong—it was because it felt right. For a little while they were a family—a family on vacation, perhaps—and they left their troubles behind.

Emir was a father to his daughters this morning, and the twins delighted at the love and affection surrounding them. Emir splashed around with Nakia, hoisted Clemira on his shoulders as she giggled in delight. And in the water with them was Amy, and he did not leave her out. They stopped for a kiss.

The pool was shaded by the palms, but the sun did not let them be. It dotted through the crisscross of leaves and glimmered on the water. It chased and it caught up and there was nothing they could do.

'Let me get a photo,' Amy said. 'For the nursery.' She wanted the girls to have a picture with their father—a picture of the three of them together and happy.

This was how it could be, Amy realised as she looked at the image on her phone, looked at the people she felt were her family.

An almost family.

It wasn't enough.

'Get the girls ready,' Emir said as they walked back inside. 'And then bring them down to breakfast.'

She blinked at the change in him, and then she understood—in a few moments they would face each other at the breakfast table, would be expected to carry on as if nothing was between them.

Emir was back to being King.

CHAPTER TWELVE

AND so the feast continued.

The birth of the new Prince demanded an extensive celebration, and Amy could see the tiredness in Natasha's eyes as she greeted the never ending stream of guests.

It was a semi-formal breakfast. There was a long, low table groaning with all the food Amy had come to love in her time there, but she was not here to socialise or to eat, but to make sure that the twins behaved. It was assumed she would have eaten before the Princesses rose.

Of course, she was starving.

Starving, her eyes told him. He watched them linger on the *sfiha* he reached for. He was at Rakhal's table, and it would be rude not to indulge, but it tasted of guilt on his tongue.

He was weak for her. Emir knew that.

And weak kings did not make good decisions.

'Have something!' Natasha insisted, sitting next to Amy as she fed the girls. 'For goodness' sake.'

'I already ate,' Amy responded. 'But thank you.'

'I insist,' Natasha said. She saw her husband's eyes shoot her a warning but she smiled sweetly back, for there was something that Rakhal did not know—something she had not had time to tell him.

When he had gone riding that morning she had taken tea on the balcony—had heard the sound of a family together, had felt the love in the air. She knew only too well the strain of being considered an unsuitable bride, yet things were changing here in Alzirz and they could change too in Alzan.

Amy did her best to forget she was hungry as she fed the twins. Did her best not to give in to the lure of his voice, nor turn her head when he spoke. She tried to treat him with the distant, quiet reverence that any servant would.

The twins were a little too loud, but very funny, smiling at their audience as they entertained, basking in the attention. As the breakfast started to conclude she wiped their faces, ready to take them back to their room and to pack for the journey home.

Not home, she reminded herself. She was returning to the palace.

With the evidence of last night in her case.

Just for a brief moment she lost focus, daydreamed for a second too long, considering the impossible as she recalled last night. Of course Clemira noticed her distraction.

Clemira demanded attention. 'Ummi!'

Amy snapped her eyes open, prayed for a futile second that no one had heard. But just in case they hadn't Nakia followed the leader as she always did.

'Ummi!'

'Amy!' She forced out the correction, tried to sound bright and matter of fact, but her eyes were filling with tears, her heart squeezing as still the twins insisted on using the Arabic word for mummy.

'I'll go and get them ready for the journey home.' She picked up Clemira, her hands shaking, grateful when Natasha stood and picked up Nakia.

Natasha was the perfect hostess, instantly realising the *faux pas* the little girls had made. Doing her best to smooth things over, she followed Amy out of the room with Nakia. But as Amy fled past the table she caught a brief glimpse of Emir. His face was as grey as the incoming storm—and there *would* be a storm. Amy was certain of it.

The tension chased her from the room. The realisation that continuing on was becoming increasingly impossible surrounded her now. She wished Natasha would leave when they reached the nursery, wished she would not try to make conversation, because Amy was very close to tears.

'I will go back and explain to them.' Natasha was practical. 'I know how difficult things can be at times, but once I explain how similar the words are...' She tried to make things better and, perhaps selfishly, yearned for Amy to confide in her. The only thing missing in her life was a girlfriend—someone from home to chat to, to compare the country's ways with. 'Anyway, it's surely natural that they would think of you in that way.'

'I'm not their mother.'

'I know.' Natasha misinterpreted Amy's tears as she cuddled Clemira into her—or perhaps she didn't. Her words were the truth. After all, she had heard them as a family that morning. 'It must be so hard for you—to detach, I mean, you've known them since the day they were born.'

'Why would it be hard for me to detach?' Amy met the Queen's eyes and frowned, her guard suddenly up. Natasha sounded as if she really did know how hard it was for her, and she must never know—no one must ever know. But Amy was suddenly certain that Natasha did, and her attempt to refute it was desperate. 'I'm a royal nanny—as Kuma is.'

Natasha knew she had meddled too far, but she stepped back a little too late. 'Of course you have to keep a professional detachment.' Natasha nodded. Amy was not going to confide in her, she realised, so she tried to salvage the conversation as best she could. 'After all, you will have your own babies one day.'

Amy was tired—so tired of women who assumed, who thought it was so straightforward, that parenthood was a God-given right. Maybe, too, she was tired of covering up, tired of saying the right thing, tired of putting others at ease as they stomped right over her heart.

She looked up at Natasha. 'Actually, I can't have children.' She watched the blush flood Natasha's cheeks and then fade till her skin was pale. She knew then that somehow Natasha knew about herself and Emir—perhaps they had given themselves away last night at the celebration? Perhaps they'd ignored each other just a touch too much? Or was their love simply visible to all?

Yes, love, Amy thought with a sob of bitterness—a bitterness that carried through to her words. 'So, yes, while it might have been a touch awkward for everyone at breakfast to hear the twins call me Ummi, for me it hurts like hell. Now...' She wanted her tears to fall in private, for Natasha was not her friend. 'If you'll excuse me...?'

'Amy—'

'Please!' Amy didn't care if it was the Queen

she was dismissing, didn't care if this was Natasha's home. She just wanted some privacy, some space. 'Can you please just leave it?'

Had she looked up she would have seen tears in Natasha's eyes too as she nodded and left her. And Natasha's eyes filled again when she took her place back at the table and saw Emir sit tall and proud, but removed.

Natasha had seen that expression before. It was the same as it had been when he had lost Hannah. Grey and strained, his features etched in grief.

As Emir looked up, as he saw the sympathy in Natasha's expression, he knew she had been told—that Amy must have somehow confided the truth.

That it was impossible for her to be Queen.

CHAPTER THIRTEEN

HE MET the day he dreaded and rose at dawn.

His prayers were deep.

Guilt lashed like a whip to his back. He had not allowed a year to pass before he touched another woman and deep was Emir's prayer for forgiveness; yet there was nothing to forgive, his soul told him. That wasn't the prayer that she needed to hear.

He could feel Hannah reaching from the grave, desperate for him to say it, for without those words how could she rest?

'I will make the best decision.'

Still it was not what she wanted; still he was forced to look deeper. Yet he dared not.

He visited the nursery. There was Amy, curled up on the sofa, reading a book with the twins. He could not look at her. Later they rode with him in the back of a car to the edge of the desert, to visit Hannah and pay their respects.

Amy sat in the vehicle and watched the trio. When he turned to walk back to the car she watched him unseen, for the windows were heavily tinted. She ached to comfort him, to say the right thing, but it was not and could never be her place.

It had been five days since they'd returned from Alzirz.

Five days of ignoring her, Emir thought as they drove back.

Five days of denial.

And a lifetime of it to look forward to.

She could see his pain, could feel his pain as they walked back into the palace, and she proved herself a liar again.

'I'm sorry today is so hard.'

He could not look at her.

'If...' She stopped herself, but with a single

word it was out there: *If it gets too tough, if things get too hard, if the night is too long...*

He turned and did not wait for the guards to open his office door; instead he strode in, saw Patel and the elders quickly shuffle some papers. But Emir knew. He did not attempt politeness, nor even ask to see what was written. He just strode to the desk and picked them up. He looked through them for a moment, a muscle flickering in his cheek as he read them.

'Sheikha Princess Jannah of Idam?' He looked to Patel—a look that demanded a rapid answer.

'She has many brothers.' Patel's voice was a touch high from fear. It was his turn to be on the receiving end of the King's anger and he did not like it one bit. 'She has many brothers. Her father too has many brothers…'

'Sheikha Noor?' Emir's voice was low, but no less ferocious.

'A strong male lineage also…' Patel's words were rapid. 'And a family of longevity.'

'Today is the anniversary of the death of Queen Hannah, and instead of being on your knees in prayer you sit and discuss the next royal intake.'

'In my defence, Your Highness, we really need to address this. The people are impatient. Today they mourn, but tomorrow they will start asking...'

'Silence!' Emir roared. It was not today that he dreaded, he realised, but tomorrow, when he must move on, and the tomorrow after that one and the next. 'You will show respect to your departed Sheikha Queen. You will give thanks for the Royal Princesses's mother.'

'Of course.'

'You do not mention the Princesses here, I note,' Emir said. 'You do not seem concerned in the least as to the new Queen's suitability for *them*.' He cursed his aide and Patel did not wait to be told to leave. Neither did the elders. Within a moment the room was cleared and he stood alone. He did not want the day over—did not want it to be tonight. For it was killing him not to go to Amy, not to draw on the comfort she would give, not to have her again and again.

He was an honourable man.

And soon he must take a wife.

He looked again to the list that had been drawn up, tried to picture himself standing with his new bride at his side while his lover, the woman he really wanted, stood next to him, holding his children as he made solemn vows.

It had never been harder to be King.

He picked up his phone. It was answered in an instant and he was grateful, for given two seconds he might have paused and changed his mind.

'Send the children's nanny to speak with me,' Emir said, and then specified, 'the English one.' He could only stand and wait to do this to her, to himself, but once, Emir needed it done this very moment. He had to bring things to a con-clusion tonight—needed a clear head with which to make his decision. And with Amy in the palace it was an impossible ask. He could not get through this night with her near and yet out of reach to him.

Not an army, only distance could hold him back from her tonight.

'Are you in trouble again?' Fatima asked the minute Amy returned from her swim with the twins.

Amy was starting to warm to Fatima, and the twins were too—she was very firm, but she was also fair and kind and, perhaps more importantly, she had grown fond of the twins. They were taking over her heart, which was something they could easily do.

'Trouble?' Amy smiled, assuming the kitchen had rung again to complain about her meal choices for the twins. Or perhaps they had made too much noise when they were swimming on such a revered day. 'Probably. Why?'

'I just took a phone call and the King wishes to speak with you immediately.'

At some level she had known this was coming. Deep down she had known it was only a matter of time before it happened. She just hadn't expected it today.

She had thought they might have this night, but she could not hope for anything as Fatima suggested that she tidy herself before she met with him, because Amy's hair was still wet from the pool.

'I don't think that will be necessary,' Amy said—there seemed no point having a mini makeover when you were about to be fired.

She looked around the nursery to the twins, who were now hungrily eating the grapes Fatima was passing to them, counting them out in Arabic as she did so.

They would be okay, Amy told herself as she took the long walk through the palace.

The guards opened the door as she approached,

and reminded her to bow her head until the King spoke.

She discarded that advice.

Amy walked in with her head held high, determined she would leave with grace. Except the sight of him, standing tall but so remote, made her want to be his lover again, to salvage what little they had. She opened her mouth to plead her case, but his eyes forbade her to speak and it was Emir who spoke first.

'You will leave late this afternoon. I have arranged all transport. That gives you some time to spend with the girls. I have a new nanny starting. She will assist Fatima.'

Yes, she'd wanted to do this with grace, but at the final hurdle she faltered—could not stand the thought of yet another woman taking care of *her* girls. 'No! You know the girls are better off with me—you said it yourself.'

'I did not realise then that they were learning

only to speak in English, that they knew nothing of our ways…'

'They would know a whole lot more if you spent more time with them. They don't need another nanny!'

'She will be more suitable. We must hold on to the ways of old.'

'What about London? What about their education and all Queen Hannah wanted for them?'

'*This* is their land.'

She really would never see them. Amy knew this was a goodbye for ever, and she forgot to be brave and strong. 'What you said before…about me being your lover…' She could not bear to leave—would give anything, even her pride, if it meant that she could stay. Because it was three times her heart was being broken here. She was losing three of the people she most loved. 'What you said about me raising the girls in London…'

'It is the type of thing men say when they want a woman in their bed. It is the type of thing a man says when his thoughts are not clear.' Completely devoid of emotion, he threw the most hurtful words at her, a round of bullets shot rapidly straight to her heart. He didn't stop firing. 'You really think I would choose *you* for that role?' He let out an incredulous laugh at the very thought. 'Here a mistress is a man's respite—a woman he can go to to relax and not be bombarded with everyday trivialities. You would be most unsuitable.'

He was right.

Amy felt the colour flood back to her cheeks, and she felt the fire in her soul return too—a fire that had been doused by the accident, that had flared only on occasion in recent times. But it was back now, and burning even more brightly, fuelling her to stand up to him.

'I *would* be a most unsuitable mistress.' She gathered her dignity and held on to it tightly, determined that she would never let it go again. She could hardly believe the offer she had made him just a few moments before and she told him why. 'I'd be a terrible mistress, in fact. I'd bombard you with news about your daughters. Every achievement, every tear I would share with you. I would busy your distinguished brain with my voice and my opinions, and…' She walked over to him—right over to where he stood. He lifted his jaw, did not look at her as she spoke, but it did not stop her. Her words told him all he would be missing. 'And there would be *no* relaxing.'

'Go!' Emir said, and still he could not look at her.

Amy knew why. He was resisting his need for her, refusing the comfort that was within his grasp.

'Go and spend time with the twins.'

'I'm going now to pack,' Amy said. 'I'll spend the afternoon at the airport.'

There was nothing left to say to him, no point pleading with him, nothing she could do for the twins. She was an employee, that was all.

But she had been his lover.

'We both know why you need me out of here today, Emir. We both know you'd be in my bed tonight, and heaven forbid you might show emotion—might tell me what's going on in the forbidden zone of your mind. You can stop worrying about that now—I'll be gone within the hour,' Amy said. 'All temptation will be removed.'

'You flatter yourself.'

'Actually, I haven't for a while. But I will from now on.'

Amy had once read that people who had been shot sometimes didn't even know, that they could carry on, fuelled by adrenaline, without realising they had been wounded. She hadn't believed it at the time, but she knew it to be true now.

She packed her belongings and rang down to arrange a car to take her to the airport. There wasn't an awful lot to pack. She'd arrived with hardly anything and left with little more—save a heart so broken she didn't dare feel it.

And because it was a royal nanny leaving, because in this land there were certain ways that had to be adhered to, Emir came out and held Clemira while Fatima held Nakia.

Amy did the hardest thing she had ever done, but it was necessary, she realised, the right thing to do. She kissed the little girls goodbye and managed to smile and not scare them. She should probably curtsy to *him*, but Amy chose not to. Instead she climbed into the car, and after a wave to the twins she deliberately didn't look back.

Never again would she let him see her cry.

CHAPTER FOURTEEN

HE HEARD the twins wail and sob late into the night. He need not have—his suite was far from the nursery—but he walked down there several times and knew Fatima could not quieten them.

'They will cry themselves out soon,' Fatima said, putting down her sewing and standing as he approached once again. She had put a chair in the hallway while she waited for the twins to give in to sleep.

Still they refused to.

He could not comfort them. They did not seem to want his comfort, and he did not know what to do.

He walked from the nursery not towards his suite but to Amy's quarters. It was a route he took in his head perhaps a thousand times each night. It was a door he fought not to open again and again. Now that he did, it was empty—the French doors had been left open to air it, so he didn't even get the brief hit of her scent. The bed had been stripped and the wardrobes, when he looked, were bare, so too the drawers. The bathroom had been thoroughly cleaned. Like a mad man, he went through the bathroom cupboards, and then back out to the bedroom, but there was nothing of her left.

He walked back to the nursery where the babies were still screaming as Fatima sewed. When she rose as he approached he told her to sit and walked into the nursery. He turned on the lights and picked up his screaming girls.

He scanned the pinboard of photos and children's paintings. There he was, and so too Hannah, and there were hundreds of pictures of the girls. But there was not a single one of Amy—not even a handprint bore her name. Emir realised fully then that she was gone from the palace and gone from these rooms—gone from his life and from his daughters' lives too.

The twins' screams grew louder, even though he held them in his arms, and Emir envied their lack of restraint and inhibition—they could sob and beat their fists on his chest, yell with indignant rage, that she was gone.

He looked out of the window to the sky that was carrying her home now. If he called for his jet possibly he could beat her, could meet her at the airport with the girls. But she was right, Emir thought with a rueful smile—she would make a terrible mistress.

She should be his wife.

'Ummi?' Clemira begged. Now she had two mothers to grieve for. He held his babies some more until finally they were spent. He put them down in one crib, but still they would not sleep, just stared at him with angry eyes, lay hiccoughing and gulping. He ran a finger down Clemira's cheek and across her eyebrows as Amy had shown him a year ago, but Clemira did not close her eyes. She just stared coolly back, exhausted but still defiant. Yes, she was a born leader.

As was Emir.

Except the rules did not allow him to be.

'I'm leaving for the desert,' he told Fatima as he left the nursery. 'The new nanny starts in two days.'

Fatima lowered her head as he walked off. She did not ask when he would return, did not insist that he tell her so she could tell the girls. That was how it was supposed to be, yet not as it should be, Emir realised.

He joined Amy in the sky—but in his helicopter.

Once in the desert, he had Raul ready his horse and then rode into the night. He was at the oasis for sunrise. The first year was over and now he must move on.

He prayed as he waited for counsel from

the wizened old man—for he knew that he would come.

'Hannah will not rest.'

The old man nodded.

'Before she died she asked that I promise to do my best for the girls.' He looked into the man's blackcurrant eyes. 'And to do the best for me.'

'And have you?'

'First I have to do the best by my country.'

'Because you are King?'

Emir nodded. 'I made that promise to my father when he died,' he said. He remembered the loss and the pain he had suffered then. His vow had been absolute when he had sworn it. 'The best for me is to marry Amy. It is the best for the girls too. But not the best for my country.' Emir told the old man why. 'She cannot have children.' He waited for the old man to shake his head, to tell him how impossible it was, to tell him there was no dilemma, that it could not be; instead he sat silent, so Emir spelt it out for him. 'She cannot give me a son.'

'And the new wife you will take can?' the old man checked.

Emir closed his eyes.

'Perhaps your new wife will give you girls too?' the old man said. 'As Queen Hannah did.'

'Without a son my lineage ends,' Emir hissed in frustration. 'Alzirz will swallow Alzan and the two lands will be become one.'

'That is the prediction,' the old man said. 'You cannot fight that.'

Emir was sick of predictions, of absolutes, of a fate that was sealed in the sand and the stars. 'It must not happen,' Emir said. He thought of his people—the people who had rejected his daughters, was his first savage thought. Yet they were not bad—they were scared. Emir knew that. He loved his people and his country so much, and they needed him as their leader. 'I cannot turn my back on them. There are rules for Alzan…'

'And for Alzirz too,' the old man said, and Emir grew silent. 'You are King for a reason.'

He reminded Emir of his teachings and Emir knew again that the year had passed and it was time for Hannah to rest, time for him to face things, to come to his decision. He stood. The old man stayed sitting.

'You will know what to do.'

He knew what to do now, and nothing could stop him.

Emir mounted his stallion and kicked him on, charged towards a land where he was not welcome uninvited. No one stopped him.

On his entering Alzirz, Rakhal's guards galloped behind and alongside him, but no one attempted to halt a king propelled by centuries of fury.

King Rakhal was alerted, and as Emir approached he saw Alzirz's King standing waiting for him outside his desert abode. His tearful wife was by his side, refusing to return to the tent;

yet she would be wise to, for both men would draw swords if they had to—both men would fight to the death for what was theirs.

Emir climbed from his horse and it was he who made the first move, reaching not for his knife but deep into his robe. He took out the two precious stones that had been sent to taunt him and hurled them at Rakhal's feet. 'Never insult me again!'

Rakhal gave a black laugh. 'How did my gift insult you? They are the most precious sapphires I could find. I had my people look far and wide for them. How could they offend?'

'They arrived on the morning of Sheikh Queen Hannah's death. The insult was for her too.' He spat in the sand in the direction of the stones and then he spat again, looking to Rakhal as he told him how it would be. 'I am marrying soon.'

'I look forward to the celebrations,' Rakhal said 'Who, may I ask, is the fortunate bride?'

'You have met her,' Emir answered. 'Amy.'

'Congratulations!' Rakhal answered, and then, because of course his wife would have told him, he smiled at Emir. 'Shouldn't you also offer congratulations to me? After all, Alzan will be mine.'

'No.' Emir shook his head.

'What? Are you considering your brother as King when you step aside?' Rakhal laughed. 'That reprobate! Hassan would not stay out of the casino or be sober long enough to take the vow.' Again Rakhal laughed. 'Congratulations to me will soon be in order.'

'Not in my lifetime,' Emir said. 'And I plan to live for a very long time. I am the King and I will die the King. Alzan will cease existing when I do.' He watched the mocking smile fade from Rakhal's face. 'I pray for a long life for your son, who will inherit all that you pass on to him. I pray that the rules are kind to him and he marries a bride who gives him healthy children. I pray for a long life for her too—for your father was lonely when his wife died, was he not? But because of your rule he could not marry again. I will pray history does not repeat for your son.' He heard Natasha really weeping now, but Rakhal stood firm.

'Your people will not be happy. Your people will never accept—'

'I will deal with my people,' Emir interrupted. 'And I will continue to pray for your son. I hope that his time in the desert proves fruitful, and hardens and prepares him for all he faces. Yes, my people will be unhappy when their King has gone. They will rise and fight as their country is taken.' He watched as for the first time Rakhal faltered when he realised the burden being placed on his newborn son, the weight both Kings carried being passed onto one. 'We are Kings, Rakhal, but without real power. For now I will rule as best I can, and do the best that I can for my children too.'

He meant it. Knew this was the right thing to do. He could no longer fight the predictions.

He rode back through the desert with rare peace in his soul. He could feel the peace in Hannah's too, for now she could rest.

Suddenly Emir halted his horse so abruptly it rose on its hind legs for a moment—or was it the shock that emanated from his master that startled the beast? Emir's realisation dawned: he had not yet discussed this with Amy. Yet surely his concern was unnecessary, he told himself. Surely no woman would refuse such a request.

But she was not from this land, and she was like no woman he knew. His last words to her had not been kind. He was back to being troubled as he realised she might not want to rule with him a people who with each passing year would grow more and more despondent. She might well prefer not to live in a land where her fertility or lack of it was a constant topic.

It dawned on him fully then—Amy might not say yes.

CHAPTER FIFTEEN

IT WAS hell being back in England.

It was lovely to see everyone, and it was good to be home, Amy told herself. Good to be at her mother's.

For about one day, seven hours and thirty-six minutes.

But when she was told by her mother again that she'd warned her not to get too attached, as if the twins were like the hamsters she'd once brought home to care for during the school holidays, Amy knew that she had to move out.

It took her a week to find a small furnished rental while she looked around for something more permanent, something that might one day feel like home. Right now her heart still lived at the palace. At night she yearned to be next to

Emir, and she still slept with one ear open for the twins. Her breasts ached as if she *were* weaning them, but she knew she had to somehow start healing—start over, start again. She'd done it once, she told herself. The next time would surely be easier. Right?

She tried to hold it together—she went out with friends, caught up with the news, bought a new London wardrobe and even went and had her hair done, in a nice layered cut with a few foils. Her friends told her she looked amazing. Those days swimming in the pool with the twins meant that she had arrived in the middle of a London winter with a deep golden tan.

She had never looked better—except her appearance didn't match the way she felt.

'You look great,' her ex fiancé told her.

If she heard it again she thought she might scream. But he'd heard she was back and wanted to catch up, and Amy was actually glad for the chance to apologise.

'For what?' he asked.

For the year of bitterness she had needlessly carried. He'd been right to end things, Amy told him.

'Are you sure about that?' he asked, before dropping her home. Fresh from a break-up with a single mum, he had revised his paternity plans and suggested that they might try again.

She *was* sure, she told him. Because it wasn't a logical love she wanted, Amy knew as she headed inside, it was an illogical one.

She knew what love was now.

Even if she did not understand it.

Even if it could never be returned.

She'd had her heart broken three times.

The accident, losing her fiancé, the aftermath—they didn't even enter the equation. They had been tiny tasters for the real grief to come.

She missed her babies, loved each little girl as fiercely as she would have loved her own. She had been there at their birth and held them every day since and she ached for them. She felt she had let Hannah down—not by sleeping with Emir, but by leaving the girls.

She was tired of being told she'd get over it—as if the love she felt didn't count, as if in a few days' times she'd wake up not missing them—but somehow she had to work out how to do just that.

She would not cry, Amy told herself. She had to keep it all together. She would look for a job next week and make some appointments—catch up on the life she'd left behind. Except as she went in her bag for her phone it was not to see if he'd called—because it had been two weeks now and still he had not—but to look at the photo of Emir and the girls that she had taken on that precious morning in Alzan.

She was horrified when she opened her bag to find that her phone was missing. Amy tipped out the contents, frantically trying to remember when she had last used her phone, positive she had taken it out with her. Perhaps she had left it at the restaurant? But, no—Amy remembered that she had sneaked a peek of the photo in the car.

It wasn't the phone that concerned her but that image of Emir, Clemira and Nakia that she could not stand to lose. It was all she had left of them.

Amy couldn't even telephone her ex to ask if he had it, because his number was in her phone. Just as she started to panic the doorbell rang. Amy ran to it, hoping he had found it, even smiling in relief as she opened the door. Her smile faded as soon as she saw who it was.

'Emir?'

There were so many questions behind that single word, but his name was all she could manage. She wasn't even sure that it was him. For a moment she even wondered if he had sent his brother, for the man standing in her doorway was the Emir she had never seen—a younger looking, more relaxed Emir—and he was smiling at her shocked expression. How dared he look so happy? How dared he look so different? For though she knew he wore suits in London, she had never seen him wear one and he truly looked breathtaking.

'Not the man you were expecting?'

'Actually, no.' She didn't have to explain herself and refused to, because even if he *had* seen her ex drop her off it was none of his business any more.

'You're a very hard person to find.'

'Am I?'

'Your mother wouldn't give me your address.'

'I wouldn't have expected her to.' Amy gave a tight shrug. 'So how *did* you find me?'

'Less than honourable ways,' he admitted.

He was powerful enough to get anything he set his mind to, and she must remember to keep her guard up around him. She could not take any more hurt, but she had to know one thing. 'Are the girls okay?'

'They're fine,' Emir said. 'Well, they miss you a lot.'

She remembered standing in his office, telling him practically the same thing, and she remembered how it had changed nothing. Yet she did ask him in—she had to know what he was here for, had to see this conversation through in the hope that she might one day move on.

'Are they here in London?'

'No.'

Emir quickly crushed that hope, but perhaps it was for the best, because she could not bear to say goodbye to them again.

'They have a new nanny. She is younger and not as rigid as Fatima. They are just starting to really settle in with her and I didn't think I should interrupt—'

'Emir, please…' She put a hand up to stop him. She really didn't need to hear how quickly and how well they were adapting to her replacement. 'I'm glad the girls are fine.'

She forced a smile and then for the first time since he'd arrived at her door remembered he was a sheikh king, she honestly forgot at times, and now that she remembered she didn't really know what to do with him.

Aware of her rather sparse furnished rental, and wondering if instant coffee would do, she remembered her manners and forced a smile for him. 'Would you like a drink?'

'I came here to talk to you.'

'You could have done that on the phone.' Except now she'd lost hers, Amy remembered. But what had seemed so devastating a few moments ago became a triviality. 'Have a seat. I'll make a drink.'

'I didn't come here for a drink.'

'Well, I'm having one.'

She headed to the fridge and opened it, grateful for the cool blast of air as she rummaged around and found some wine and then looked for glasses. She was glad for something to do—

needed to have her back to him for a couple of moments as she composed herself. Amy did not want her broken heart on clear display to him, for she could be hurt so easily.

'What are you thinking?' Emir asked, the tiny kitchen area shrinking as he stepped in.

'Do you really want to know?'

'I really want to know.'

'That it's just as well this is a screwtop bottle because I don't have a corkscrew...'

'Amy!'

'And I'm wondering what happened to all the people who made the corks.' She was, and she was also wondering if the trees they came from were called cork trees, because it was safer than thinking about the man who was in her home, the man who was standing right behind her now. She knew that if she turned around it would be to a man she could not resist.

'What else are you thinking?'

'That it is cruel that you are here,' Amy said.

'That I don't want to be your mistress.' She stopped pouring the wine. She was making a mess of it anyway. Her eyes were filling with tears and she couldn't really see; she screwed her eyes closed as his hand touched her arm and swore to be strong as he turned her around. 'And I'm thinking how right I was to leave—that I don't want to be with you.'

'I don't believe that,' he said.

And his mouth was there, and already she was weakening. That in itself forced her to be strong, made her look into his eyes to speak. 'I wouldn't even want to be your wife.'

'I don't believe that either.'

'I mean it.' She reminded herself that she did. 'As I've said before, if you were my husband and they were my children I'd have left ages ago.'

'I told you that there were reasons I could not be the father I wanted to be for them, but those reasons are gone now.'

She shook her head. 'I don't want you, Emir.'

'You *do* want me.'

He was so bloody arrogant, so assured…so right.

'No.'

'That's not what your body is saying.'

He ran a hand down her arms, then removed it. She shivered, for only his touch could warm her.

'And it's not what I see in your eyes.'

So she hid them, lowered her head, and because the bench was behind her and she could not step back she lifted her hands to push him—yet she dared not touch. 'Just go, Emir,' she begged. 'I can't think straight when you're around.'

'I know,' Emir said.

She shook her head, because how could he know how it felt? After all, he was standing calm and controlled and she was a trembling mess.

'I know how impossible it is to make a wise decisions when love clouds the issue.'

She did look up then, shocked to hear him speak of love. A gasp came from her lips when he spoke next, when he said what no king should. 'I have been considering abdicating.'

'*No.*' He must not think it—let alone say it. She knew from her time in Alzan the implications, knew how serious this was, but Emir went on undaunted. This distant man invited her closer, and not just to his body, but to his mind; he pulled her in so her head was on his chest as he told her, shared with her his hell.

'Whenever I saw the twins laughing and happy, or crying and sad, I wanted them to come first— I did not want to rule a country that is disappointed by my daughters, that does not celebrate in their birthday, that will only be appeased by a son. When I am with my daughters all I want to do is step down...'

'You can't.'

'I am not sure that I want to rule a country where I cannot change the rules. I'm not sure I want to give the people the son they want just to pass the burden on to him.' He shook his head.

'No, I will not do that to my son.' He lifted her chin and looked into the eyes of the woman he loved and was completely sure. 'I love you, and I cannot lose the woman I love again.'

And it was right, Amy thought, that he acknowledged Hannah—even right that the love he felt should be compared to the love he had had for the Queen. And it was said so nicely that she could not help but cry.

'And neither can I put Clemira and Nakia through it again,' he went on. 'You have made my daughters so happy. They call you their mother—which is how it will be.' He watched her shake her head at the impossibility of it all. 'As soon as you left I wanted to get on a plane, but I knew I had to think this through. I will rule Alzan as best as I can in my lifetime, and if the people grow hostile, if things get too hard for you there, then the country will see less of their leader—for I will divide my time between there and here.'

'No…' Amy said, but he was close, and she was weak whenever Emir was around.

'Yes,' he said, and held her tight. 'Anyway, we will have time to work things out.' He could not help but tease, watching the colour spread up her cheeks as he spoke. 'No one needs to find out for a while yet that you cannot have children.'

'I told Natasha.' She thought his features would darken with surprise, but instead he smiled.

'I know you did.'

'I was just tired of everyone assuming…'

'I know.' And he was smiling no longer. 'I confronted Rakhal. I have told him my position.'

'What did he say?'

'That Alzan will be his.' Emir shrugged. 'I pointed out that if he does outlive me and inherit, one day it will be his son's too.' His voice was forboding, but the loathing was not aimed at her. She knew that. 'If Rakhal takes it upon himself to inform my people that you cannot have a child…' his features were dark, and now he was not smiling '…he will have *me* to deal with.'

'I can't marry you, Emir,' Amy said. 'I can't stand knowing that I'm going to disappoint your people.' That he loved her so much brought her both comfort and fear. That he would leave his country's future in darkness for her was almost more than she could take.

'It is not your burden to carry,' Emir said. 'I was coming to this decision even before the twins were born. I was already considering this. For Hannah's heart was so weak I could never have asked her to be pregnant again. This is not of your making. We have time before the people know—time to work out how best to tell them.'

He was doing his best to reassure her, but even if his decision was right, she knew the pain behind it.

'I can't do it, Emir.'

'You can with me by your side. I will shield you as I will shield the twins. You will be a wonderful queen,' Emir said. 'The people could not have better.'

'They could.'

'No.'

He meant it.

Every word of it.

His heart was at peace with the decision he had made. He would do everything he could for his people, but his heart belonged to his girls and he was strong enough to end the impossible burden, to cease the madness. He would not place that burden on a child of his.

And here it was—the illogical love that she wanted. Love was a strange thing: it made you both strong and weak. Strong enough to stand by your convictions... Weak enough maybe to give in.

Except this was Emir, and even if she forgot at times he was King this was her life and it would be in the spotlight.

As she wrestled with indecision the doorbell

rang. She opened it to the man she had once thought she loved, and blinked at the phone he held out in his hand.

'Thank you.'

She saw him look over her shoulder to where Emir was standing, saw the raising of his eyebrows, and then without a word he turned and Amy closed the door. She was nervous to turn around and face the man she knew she loved and would love for ever. But she had to be strong, had to say no, and that slight pause had given her a moment to regroup.

'I left my phone…' She felt his black eyes on hers and couldn't quite meet them. 'We went out before…'

'I saw you return,' Emir said. 'I was waiting in my car for you. Now, we were talking about—'

'Nothing happened,' Amy broke in. 'He just wanted…'

'I do not care.' She frowned, because surely

he *should* care. 'We were discussing our marriage—'

'Emir!' she interrupted him. 'My ex-fiancé just came to the door, you know we've been out together tonight, and you don't *care*?' She couldn't believe what she was hearing. 'You don't have questions?'

'None,' Emir said.

She was less than flattered. A bit of jealousy wouldn't go amiss—after all, she *had* just been out with her ex.

'Am I supposed to take it as a compliment that you trust me so much? For all you know—'

'You could take a thousand lovers, Amy.' It was Emir who interrupted now. Emir who walked to where she stood. 'But each one would leave you empty. Each one would compare poorly to me.'

'You're so sure?'

'Completely,' Emir said. 'And you could sit through a hundred dinners and dates and your mind would wander even as the first course was served.' He stood right in front of her, looked down at her, and spoke the absolute truth. 'Your mind would wander straight back to me,' he said.

And, damn him, he was right. Because tonight all she had thought of was Emir, her efforts to concentrate and to listen had been half-hearted at best.

'And when you were kissed,' he said, and put his mouth right up to hers, 'you would crave what another man could not deliver. Because my mouth knows best what to do.'

She closed her eyes, opened her mouth to deny him. For there must be no future for them. She was going to say that she would find love again—except his tongue slid into her protesting mouth and he gave her a taste, and then he drew his head back, warned her again of the life she would lead if she did not say yes.

'You would miss me for ever.'

'No,' she begged, though she knew he spoke the truth.

'You would regret the decision for the rest of your days.'

'No,' Amy insisted, though she knew he was right.

'We will be married,' he concluded, through with talking. It had taken what felt like a lifetime to come to his decision, and now that he had he wanted it sealed.

He pulled her tighter to him, so close she could hear his heart—not galloping, but steady, for he knew he was right.

His hand lifted her chin and he looked down at her mouth. 'There are so many kisses we have not had.'

He lowered his mouth and tender were the lips that met hers in an unhurried kiss that reminded her of nothing—for this side of him she had not met.

'This is the kiss I wanted to give you one morning when I saw you walking in the gardens.' His mouth claimed her for another brief moment. He ran his hands down to her waist and his lips tasted of possession and promise for later. Then he he let her go. 'That was the kiss I wanted to greet you with when you joined the party.'

'What is this?' She would not cry in front of him. She had promised herself. Yet she was failing. 'Guess the kiss?'

'Yes,' he said, and she started to cry.

He held her again and his mouth drank her tears. He held her as he had wanted to, comforted her as he had wanted to after the breakfast, when Clemira had said *Ummi* and her heart had ached for a baby of her own. He held her as had wanted to that day.

'You will never face it alone again,' he promised, for he knew his kiss had taken her back to that day.

Then he kissed her again, both hands on her face, and it tasted of regret. She was leaving him again. They were back at the palace and he was letting her go. His arms were around hers and his tongue met hers. He was ferocious as he rewrote that moment—he kissed her back to his world. Then he kissed her hard and with intent, and *this* was a kiss she recognised. His tongue was lavish in its suggestion and he pulled her into him, to let her feel his want. His hands moved over her body. This was a kiss that could lead only to one thing.

Except he stopped.

He looked down to her mouth, which was wet and wanting. He did not believe in negotiation—not when he knew that he was right. He *would* get his way. 'You will return to Alzan and we will be married.'

'You don't just *tell* me!' Amy said. 'And that's hardly a proposal. You're supposed to get down on one knee.'

'Not where I come from,' Emir said.

He took her hand and held it over his erection. She kept her palm flat, but that did not deter him. He moved her hand up and down, till her fingers ached from not holding him, till all she wanted was to slide down his zipper and free him.

Free *them*.

'You can say yes,' Emir said, 'or you can kiss it goodbye if you care to.'

She could not help but smile as his usually excellent English wavered.

'You mean, kiss it *all* goodbye.'

'No,' Emir said. 'I mean exactly what I said.' And he pulled her into him. His mouth found her ear. 'Either way I bring you to your knees.'

And he would, because she could not be without him.

'Say yes, Amy.'

'I can't.'

'Then you can't have me.'

He confused her, because he kissed her again.

He kissed her mouth when still she questioned. He kissed her eyes closed when she tried to look at all that lay ahead. He kissed her until she was in the moment—kissed her all the way to her unmade bed. He did not bring her to her knees; instead he lay her down and removed every piece of her clothing.

First he took off her shoes, and when she sat with her arms by her sides he raised them.

'Emir...'

'Tell me to stop and I will.'

Her hands stayed in the air as he took off her top.

'Tell me we should not be together,' Emir said as he unhooked her bra, 'and I will go.'

And she felt his eyes on her breasts and she wanted his mouth to be there, but still she stayed silent, so he unzipped her skirt and pushed her back on the bed. When he pulled at the hem she did not lift her hips to help him. He stared down at her and it did not deter him. Instead he undressed himself.

He took off his jacket and placed it over a chair,

took ages with each shoe, and as he pulled off his socks Amy found her toes curling.

'You do not get me till you say yes.' With a cruel lack of haste he removed his tie and unbuttoned his shirt. He gave her plenty of time to halt things but still she did not and he slid off his trousers and hipsters and stood over her, naked. 'I can't hear you, Amy.'

'Because I haven't said anything,' came her response, but this time when he tugged at her skirt she did lift her hips. How could she not say yes to him? How could she not be his wife? She tried to look to the future, when she would surely regret this decision, but *yes* waited to spill from her mouth.

He took off her panties so she was naked, and still she would not give in.

Emir kneeled between her legs, kissed up one thigh and then back down, and then he turned his attention to the other one till she writhed beneath him, wanting him there at her centre. He didn't play fair. He played mean. He lifted his head and focussed instead on himself, and she watched, fascinated, desperate. He stroked himself right there at her entrance and she watched, wanted. He would make her comply.

'I can't wait for ever,' he warned.

And he was right. There would never be a better lover. Always her mind would return to him. She heard his breath quicken. She wanted him more than she wanted her sanity and she hated this game he was playing.

'You can't seduce me into saying yes.'

'I can.'

He could.

He actually could.

'Yes,' she begged, for she wanted it to be ended.

'Manners?' How cruel was his teasing.

'I've forgotten them!' she screamed, and then screamed again as he drove into her.

Fierce was the passion that filled her. He did not stop for a second to let her think, did not let her draw breath to reconsider. He had her and he would keep her. Each buck inside Amy told her that. Each pounding thrust confirmed she was his and Amy knew that was what she wanted.

'Please…' she sobbed, her legs coiling around him, possessing him, locking him in while ensuring his release.

She gave in as he did—gave in to the ultimate pleasure, lost in the throes of an orgasm that sealed their union as they pulsed together in time, lost with the other and returned together, lying with each other as they would now every night.

And Emir slept as he never had, in an untroubled sleep, for he knew that this was right.

Except Amy could not rest beside him. She heard every car that passed and listened to the rain battering the window in the early hours of the morning. She was petrified about what she'd agreed to.

She was going to be Queen.

CHAPTER SIXTEEN

'You need to come home,' was his answer when she told him her fears, and she knew that he was right—knew that Alzan was where she wanted to be.

They did not stay long in London. Just long enough to sort out her things and for Amy to try and convince her mum, who would fly to Alzan for the wedding, that she knew what she was doing, that it would all be okay.

And how could they not be okay? she asked herself. For it felt so right to have Emir by her side.

The journey home was a blur—the luxurious plane a mere mode of transport that allowed her to follow her heart. Even the people cheering the arrival of their King and soon to be new Sheikha

Queen did not really register. But for all it was
a blur, for all her mind was too busy to take in
every detail, Amy would never forget her return
to the palace.

He held her hand as they walked through the
foyer where he had *not* kissed her goodbye, as
they walked up the stairs—together this time—
and then to the nursery. Emir let go of her hand,
stepped in first, and she walked in quietly behind and smiled at the delighted reaction when
the twins saw him. They were playing with their
dolls' house, making everything right in a world
where they could, but their beloved toy was instantly forgotten. Their father was back and that
was all the girls needed to know—and then they
saw her.

'Ummi!' It was Nakia who squealed it first and
Clemira frowned, glanced at her sister and chastised her, for she had learnt that word was bad.

And then Clemira looked over to where her
little sister was pointing and when she saw who

was there she forgot to be the leader; she just burst into tears and took first steps towards Amy.

'It's okay.' Amy realised how much she had been hurting because her pain was gone the second she picked up Clemira. Poor Nakia stood too, but her legs didn't know how to walk yet, so she burst out crying too, and cried some more when Amy picked her up. Overwhelmed, the twins cried till they were smiling, kissing her face because Amy was crying too. She looked to Emir and it was the closest to tears she had ever seen him.

He had lost so much—his parents, his wife and almost Amy. That he could trust in love again was a feat in itself, and his decision was the right one, Amy told herself as she held his new family.

How could this be wrong?

Yet Amy awoke on the morning of her wedding with dread in her heart. She understood why Emir had been unable to make his decision when love was around, for when he was close, when he was near, it felt so *right* that they marry, that love was the solution. But Emir had spent the eve of his wedding in the desert, and without him it was far more than pre-wedding jitters Amy was struggling with. This morning she didn't even have the twins to keep her busy, for they were being readied for the wedding by the new nanny.

She felt as if she were cheating the people.

The maid came in and opened the window and the room was filled with humid desert air. Amy felt as if it was smothering her as she tried to swallow the ripe fruit that had been picked at dawn in the desert and prepared and served to her.

As was the tradition for the future Queen of Alzan.

The maids watched as she drank fertility potions from huge goblets and with every mouthful Amy felt sicker. Each taste of bridal tradition choked her and reminded her of the cheat and liar she was.

She bathed and had her make-up and hair done. Her eyes were lined with kohl and her cheeks and lips rouged. But she could see the pallor in her face and the guilt in her eyes as blossom was pinned into her hair— 'For innocence,' the maiden explained. Amy closed her eyes on another lie as she remembered the love they had already made.

A dress of pale gold slithered over her head and she thought of her mother who, though there for the wedding, was stressed. She had done all she could to dissuade Amy. As late as last night she had warned her daughter of the mistake she was making, had offered to take her home; she had told Amy that she was taking on too much, that though the country was cheering at the union now it would soon turn against her, and maybe in time her husband would too.

'No.' Amy was adamant. 'He loves me.'

Yet she felt guilty accepting that love. What should be the happiest day of her life was blighted by the knowledge that she could never be the Queen the people really wanted.

And now the final touches. She could hear the excitement and anticipation building in the streets outside, for the wedding was to take place in the gardens and the people had gathered around the palace.

'The people are happy,' the maiden said as a loud cheer went up.

'It is King Rakhal and Queen Natasha, arriving,' a younger maiden informed the busy room, watching the proceedings from the window. 'They have the young Prince with them.' She looked to Amy and smiled. 'They won't be able to gloat over us for much longer.'

And now the maiden tied a necklace around her throat which had a small vial at the end of it. Amy knew even before the maiden told her that it was for fertility, for Clemira and Nakia had received a similar necklace in the desert. Emir's response then had been brusque, but the maiden was more effusive as she arranged it around Amy's throat.

'It is to ensure that the sands remain as Alzan.' She placed it over the scar on Amy's throat and Amy could feel her rapid pulse beating there against the vial, could hear the cheers from the people of Alzan building outside, she could feel the sweat removing her carefully applied make-up as the humid desert air made it impossible to breathe.

'Amy?'

She heard the concern in the young maiden's voice, and the shocked gasps from the others as they saw how much she was struggling.

'I can't do this,' was all Amy remembered saying as she slid to the ground.

CHAPTER SEVENTEEN

'SHE is late.'

Emir heard the whispers in the crowd and stared fixedly ahead. Though outwardly calm and in control, he was kicking himself, for he should not have left her alone last night. He knew the reason Amy was late was because she was reconsidering the union. He realised that perhaps, for her, it was too much too soon—after all, his decision had been more than a year in the making. But Emir knew he could not lose his love to a prediction, knew he was right, and he would go now and tell her the same.

'That is not necessary,' Patel informed him. 'She is better now, apparently. They have given her salts to smell and some fluids to drink and she will soon be on her way.'

As Amy approached she reminded Emir of the first time he had met her—pale and quiet but somehow strong. She had helped him so much at that heartbreaking time and he wanted to help *her* now, wanted to take her away from the gathered crowd, to talk to her, soothe and reassure her, but of course it was impossible.

'You are okay?' Emir checked as she joined him at his side, and his hand found hers.

She was touched at the gesture, for he had told her that today was duty, that feelings would not be on display—for in Alzan love usually came later.

Not today.

'Nervous,' Amy admitted, which was perhaps the understatement of the century.

The magnitude of what was about to take place had hit her again as she'd walked through the fragrant gardens and seen the crowd, and she had thought she might pass out again. There was Hassan, the reprobate brother, standing tall and silent by his brother's side. King Rakhal and Natasha were there too, regal and splendid, but she'd barely glanced at them. First she had looked to the twins, dressed in pale lemon and sitting on the grass holding flowers, but though she'd melted at the sight of them today it was Emir who won her heart a thousand times over.

His robe was pale gold too, as was the *kafeya* on his head, and she was overwhelmed by such male beauty, by the curve of his lips that barely smiled as they greeted her but that would caress her mouth tonight. She ached for tonight, to be in the desert with him, but of course there were formalities first.

For a country so steeped in tradition, the wedding was surprisingly simple.

'He asks,' Emir translated, 'if you agree to this union.'

'Yes,' Amy said, and then remembered and answered for the judge. *'Na'am.'*

'He asks that you will obey me.'

He saw the slight pursing of her lips, for they had discussed this a few times.

She pressed her thumb into his palm, to remind him of the million subclauses to her agreement, and then she answered, *'Na'am.'*

'He asks will you nurture the fruits of our union?' Emir saw the tears fill her eyes and he wanted to hold her, but all he could do was press his own thumb to her palm to remind her that this was right.

She could not look beyond his shoulder to where King Rakhal stood, and beside him Natasha, so she looked to her soon to be husband and answered him. The press of his thumb was a reminder of just how much this man loved her. *'Na'am.'*

The judge spoke for a few moments and she waited, then Emir's hand was in the small of her back, telling her to turn around.

'What happens now?' Amy asked.

'We go back to the palace.'

'Back?' Amy asked. 'But the wedding…?'

'We are married,' Emir said, and then he broke with tradition.

Even if it was brief she felt his arms around her, and the soft warmth of his mouth as Emir kissed his bride. It was not the cough of the elders that halted them but the two little girls who protested at the lack of attention.

Back to the palace they walked, holding one twin each, and she watched as Emir glanced up to the sky. She knew he was telling Hannah she could rest now, that the girls would be looked after as she had wanted.

And they would be.

Amy wanted to be alone with him, wanted their night in the desert, but first came more formalities—a sumptuous meal and endless speeches. Finally it was Rakhal's turn to speak, and Amy felt her hand tighten on the glass she was holding. She wondered what barb was about to be delivered—not that she would know it when it came, for the speeches were in Arabic. Emir would translate for her.

She took a deep breath as Rakhal addressed the room, realised her fingers were suddenly tight around Emir's for he squeezed her hand back.

'My wife predicted this.' Rakhal spoke in English and Amy's head jerked up. 'She said she knew on the day she met you,' he said. 'It was the day of my father's passing.'

Amy blinked, because that was a long time ago—long before she had had feelings for Emir. Or had she? She remembered that time. Emir had gone to offer his farewell and she had spoken briefly with Natasha. She had been so confused and bitter then, so angry with Emir for the distance he put between himself and his daughters.

'I said she was wrong.' Rakhal looked at the new Queen of Alzan. 'And I said she was wrong again at my son's naming ceremony. But this is one prediction that has been proved right.' Rakhal looked to Emir. 'Your Highness, I congratulate you on your wedding.' He spoke in Arabic, some words she recognised—long life, good health—and then again he spoke in English. 'The Kingdom of Alzirz celebrates with you today.'

How hard it was to smile as he raised a glass to them.

Hard too, to make small talk with Natasha a while later, for she was so determined to be friendly.

'You look wonderful.' Natasha smiled, but Amy could not help but be cool in her responses—could not so easily manage the feigned politeness between the rivals. 'Rakhal tells me you are honeymooning in London?'

'That's right.'

'With the girls?'

'Of course,' Amy said through gritted teeth.

'When you return we must get the children together, Clemira is so taken with Tariq, and...'

'We'll see.' Amy gave a tight smile. 'Now, if you'll excuse me...'

She turned straight into the chest of Emir and he rescued her with a dance. 'You will be polite,' Emir warned her. 'You will be pleasant.'

'I *am* being.'

'No.' He had seen the ice behind her smile as she spoke with Queen Natasha. 'When a queen speaks to you...'

'I'm a queen now too.'

He smiled down at her angry eyes. 'I will speak with you later. For now I will tell you to be polite.'

'I don't get it, Emir,' she bristled.

It annoyed her how well Emir and Rakhal were getting on tonight—oh, she knew it was all for show, but still it riled her. She put it aside, for it seemed impossible to hold a grudge on this night. The whole palace was alive with celebration, there were parties in the streets outside, and though she ached to be alone in the desert with Emir, to be with her new husband, it was the best night of her life.

Amy allowed herself simply to enjoy it right up to the end, when she accepted a kiss to her hand from Rakhal and, as instructed, smiled and chatted briefly to Natasha as they prepared to leave for the desert. Then it was time to say goodbye to the twins.

God, but she loved them. Nakia was now literally following in her big sister's footsteps, toddling too, and both loved calling out 'Ummi'. They would always know about their real mother, but it was bliss not to correct them, just to scoop them into her arms. She did it now, kissed their little faces and told them she would see them tomorrow.

She feared the wedding night in the desert more than a little—always felt as if the desert knew something she didn't, as if somehow it was a step ahead of them.

'It's dark.'

The last time she had been there the sands had been lit by a huge moon, and there had been stars, but tonight the desert was clouded—not that Emir seemed concerned.

'There will be rain, which is good,' he said. 'After rain comes new growth.'

The rain met them as they landed—a driving rain that had the helicopter flounder for a moment, a pelting rain that soaked through her gown. As she stepped into the tent maidens were waiting, wrapping her in shawls, and a feast was laid out for them. There were a thousand things to get through when all she wanted was to be alone with him, to speak with him. Emir must have sensed that, for he dismissed the maidens and took her into his arms.

'Should I be offended,' Emir asked, 'that my wife did not enjoy her wedding day?'

'I loved it, Emir.' She looked up to him. 'Every moment of it.'

'Every moment?'

'I struggle to be polite to Natasha and Rakhal. I understand that I have to be, that without communication…' She did not want to talk about them on her wedding night but, yes, she might have been a little rude. 'I struggle sometimes to stay quiet when I believe there is injustice.'

'I *had* worked that out,' Emir said. 'I know there is much on your mind. All day I have wanted to speak with you. There is something you need to know, but there has not been a suitable moment.'

'Oh!' Amy had been about to say the same thing. 'Emir, there is something—'

'Amy,' he interrupted, for his news was too important not to share. 'You know I spent last night in the desert? Usually the night before the King marries is a time for feasting and celebrating; instead I spent that time speaking with Rakhal.'

'And you didn't pull your swords?'

He heard the teasing in her voice. 'Rakhal listened to all I said to him that day—he thought long and hard about it and though things have worked out for him, though he is happy, he does not want the burden he carried to be passed on to his son. He agrees that we are Kings without power unless we make our own rules for our own lands.' Emir picked up the vial that hung around her throat, knew the terrible pressure that had been placed on her. 'Our decision will be refuted by the elders, of course, but with both Kings in full agreement there will be no going back.'

'I don't understand?'

'The predictors are wrong,' Emir said. 'Alzan and Alzirz are two strong and proud countries. It is time for them to break free from the rules of old. Of course the people and the elders will challenge this. They believe...'

'Emir!' That whooshing sound was back in

her ears, 'Emir, wait!' Anguished eyes looked up to him. 'I did enjoy today, every moment of it, and if I seemed distracted at times...' Amy took a deep breath. 'I didn't faint from nerves.' She still couldn't take the news in, had been reeling from it all day. 'Well, maybe a bit. But when the palace doctor examined me...' She'd never thought she'd hear herself say these words. 'I'm pregnant, Emir.' Amy was crying now, and not just a little bit. 'I had him retake the test and he is certain—it would seem that first night...'

'But you said it was impossible.' It was Emir who didn't understand.

'There was always a slim chance, apparently,' Amy explained. 'I just didn't hear that and neither did my fiancé. And I never went back to the doctor to properly discuss things.'

Emir held her as she cried. The news was as shocking as it was happy, and it took a moment for it to sink in.

'The rules might not need to change. I might have a son,' Amy said.

And he held the bride whom he loved, come what may, and he loved her all over again.

'Soon we will be able to find out what I'm having.'

'There is no need to find out,' Emir said. 'For whatever we are given we will love. The rules *will* change.' Emir's voice was firm. 'Clemira is a born leader, that much I know, and Nakia will be a wonderful support for her. It is right she be second in line.'

'But the predictions!'

'Are just that,' Emir said, and he looked to the woman who had healed his black and tortured heart, the woman who had swept into his office and challenged his way of thinking, and he could not believe what he had. His instinct was to kiss her, to hold her and soothe her fears, and then he paused for just a moment as the news truly started to hit him. And he told her why the predictions were surely wrong. 'They did not factor in that a king might fall in love.'

EPILOGUE

'HE is beautiful,' Emir said.

Amy could not stop looking at her newborn son—could scarcely believe that she was holding her own baby in her arms. Just feeling him there, she knew all the hurts of the past were forgotten, the pain of the last twenty-four hours simply deleted as she looked down into his dark eyes.

'Are you sure he's mine?' Amy teased, because he was completely his father's son. She looked up to Emir and he kissed her gently, and she was bathed in a happiness made richer because he loved her and his daughters, with or without the gift of a son.

He took the baby in his arms and held him for a long moment, and Amy could see the pride and also the pain on his strong, proud features, for he was surely remembering the bittersweet time when he'd last held a tiny infant.

'I don't want to miss a moment of his life,' Emir said. 'I missed way too much of the twins' first year.' He closed his eyes in regret.

'Emir, there was a reason.' She understood that now.

'Every time I saw them, every time I held them, all I wanted was to do what was best for them, and yet I had the responsibility to put the future of my country first.'

'It must have been agony.'

'I was made better knowing they were looked after by you. When you left, when it was Fatima, when the ways of old were being adhered to, I knew I could not rule a country that rendered my daughters worthless. It worked in the past, but not now,' Emir explained. 'Yet it was a decision that required distance.'

'It did,' Amy agreed. 'I wish you could have spoken with me...' Her voice trailed off, because

Emir was right. It was a decision that could only have been reached alone. 'It's all worked out.' She looked at her sleeping baby. 'The rules don't even have to change.'

'They do,' Emir said. 'For I never want my son to have to make a choice like the one I was forced to make. The predictors were wrong: the two countries are better separated. I am glad I have a son for many reasons, but it will prove once and for all that we are doing this because it is right rather than necessary. The people will love him as they now love the girls—as they love you.'

The changes of the past few months had been less tumultuous than Amy had feared. The old Bedouin man had laughed when Rakhal and Emir consulted him, had shrugged and shaken his head when they'd said that the predictions were wrong. But the people in the main had accepted it, reassured that their two Kings were united and strong in their decision. And even before they'd found out that Amy was expecting a baby they had cheered for the twins, and a newspaper had celebrated with a headline about the future Queen Clemira.

'Your mother should be here any time,' Emir said, because as soon as Amy had gone into labour Emir had organised a plane for her.

Amy could not wait to see her mother's face when, after all the anguish, she got to hold her grandson.

'Shall I bring the girls in to meet their new brother?' Emir asked, handing his son back to her outstretched arms.

'Okay,' Amy said, excited about their reaction. She smiled as he brought the girls in. She loved them so much—every bit as much as the baby in her arms. She had loved them from the moment they were born. She watched Nakia's face light up when she saw her new brother. She was completely entranced, smothering him with kisses, but Clemira seemed less than impressed.

She looked at him for a moment or two and then wriggled down off the bed and toddled off. Following her sister's lead, soon so too did Nakia. Emir called for the nanny to take them back to the playroom.

'Do you think she is jealous?' Emir asked, taking the now sleeping baby and placing him in his crib, then climbing onto the bed beside her. 'She barely looked at him.'

'It's early days,' Amy said. There was no nicer place in the world than to be in bed next to Emir with their baby sleeping by their side. 'I'm surprised, though. She was so taken with Tariq. I guess it will take a bit of getting used…' She did not finish her sentence because it was taken over by a yawn.

Emir pulled her in. 'You need to rest.'

'Stay.'

'Of course,' Emir said. 'But you must sleep while you have the chance. The next weeks will be busy—your family arriving and the naming ceremony… And Natasha has rung and wants to come over before then. She is so looking forward to seeing the baby.'

Amy smiled, half dozing. All was well in her world as she rested safe in his arms. She would look forward to Natasha's visit—they were firm friends now and met often. Their children delighted in playing together.

'I'd love to see her, and Clemira will be thrilled to see Tariq…' Her voice trailed off again, but for a different reason. An impossible thought formed between waking and sleep. 'Emir?'

'Rest,' he told her, his eyes closed, but Amy couldn't.

'If Clemira is still as taken with Tariq in…oh, say in twenty years or so…'

She looked up and his eyes opened. The frown that had formed faded as a smile broke onto his face. 'That would make things incredibly complicated.'

'Really?'

'Or incredibly simple.' He kissed the top of her head. 'Sleep now,' he said. 'It is not something we are going to consider or force. That is not a decision we will ever make for them.'

'But if it *did* happen?' Amy pushed. 'Then the countries would become one again?'

'Perhaps,' Emir said.

She closed her eyes and stopped thinking about the future, relished the present.

Emir was the one who broke the silence, the possibility perhaps still on his mind.

'Maybe I was wrong?' Emir said, pulling her in closer, feeling absolute peace in his once troubled heart. 'Who am I to say that when the predictions were made, they did not factor in love?'

* * * * *